NOT BY THE BOOK

THE PENCIL PRO

Roni Rosenthal

Not by the Book – The Pencil Pro
Text Copyright @2018 By Roni Rosenthal
All rights reserved

Published by The Pencil Pro
www.ThePencilPro.com

Library of Congress Control Number: 2018943166

ISBN 13: 978-0-9792-8004-7 (paperback)
ISBN 13: 978-0-9792-8005-4 (ebook)

This book is dedicated to my mom, Hadass Rosenthal, who taught me that creativity has no boundaries.

Idea Contributors:
Shachar Gazit Rosenthal
Lior (Kiki) Gazit Rosenthal

NOTE FROM THE AUTHOR

A man slowly walked down the hill enjoying the beautiful sunny day.

Something was bothering him. He couldn't figure out why the physics model he had devised worked one way and not the other. What could he do to change it, was the question.

He turned left and entered a beautiful orchard filled with apple, orange, and some lemon trees. He took a deep breath inviting all those smells to fill his nostrils.

He picked an apple and sat down beneath the tree. The wind blew and rustled the leaves. He looked up to the leaf while admiring the whisper of nature.

Suddenly, the wind blew harder and an apple fell down and hit his head. It hurt. He stood up, confused.

"Aha," he cried in joy. Later, he would call this *"gravity."*

"Aha" moments like those did not just happen to Isaac Newton.

Other geniuses called it "Eureka" and "the tipping point."

In fact, we all have this ability to create breakthrough ideas. Those "aha" moments happen to each and every one of us at any given time.

Yes, those "aha" moments opened the gate to the greatest innovations in medicine, science, biology, technology and other fields.

Have you ever wondered what was the exact "aha" moment that lead to the greatest innovations of the world? What was the spark that caused famous innovators to understand that the wheel should be round, electricity is the next step, and the smart phone is exactly what's missing?

If one wanted to be successful in the 20th century, he or she had to master the 3Rs: Reading, writing, and arithmetic. The shift that came with the 21st technology century determines that in order to be successful today, you must have skills, known as the 4Cs: creativity, critical thinking, communication, and collaboration.

In order to be successful today, you must be creative and you must generate original ideas, which is why my collaborators and I have created a system to get your mind thinking in different ways. To get your mind sharp...like the end of a pencil.

The Pencil Pro was launched as a pilot program during the summer of 2016. The success was immediate. *The Pencil Pro* aims to promote original thinking and to empower the brain with creative thinking by using tools that my collaborators and I have developed.

Our model: **"Be Empowered with Creativity"** aims to spark

"aha" moments and to ignite creativity and critical thinking in the mind.

Your mind is the fuel, but only creative thinking can really get you flying.

Our model and exercises, which were carefully crafted are useful for each and every one of us. As you'll see in this book, CEOs, project managers, scientists, IT engineers, real-estate agents, lawyers, and others have been active participants of *The Pencil Pro*.

Creativity—especially creative thinking—helps us make a change whether at work or in our personal lives. Original thinking helps us find solutions to complex problems or improve an existing product by simply taking a different approach or looking at the problem from a different angle. As we have learned in life, from every crisis a new solution arises, and from every solution a new set of problems is born. Those are the moments that have changed our lives and opened up new opportunities for us. Those are the moments when men and women see the development of an issue and took the time to define the problem and reach that "aha" moment of life-changing solution making.

In this book, you will find the original posts and comments of our participants at the pilot project. We've changed their names and identities to protect their privacy. In addition, the original Facebook page is no longer available.

You're about to enter the secrets behind the scenes of *The Pencil Pro*.

CHAPTER 1

A quick glance at the clock.

Three minutes to go on stage.

My stomach churns as I am waiting to give my presentation. *I shouldn't have eaten that last slice of pizza,* I think idly. I try to focus, to bring myself back to the here and now.

I must concentrate. Keep my thoughts together.

I peek behind the heavy red curtains. The lights are still on and people are searching for their seats. I can hear their murmurs and shuffling.

What am I doing here? Am I really putting my project up to the test?

This is my second time giving this presentation. The first time was at my school in front of a friendly crowd. They cheered for me and laughed at my jokes, but this time I know no one in the auditorium.

And the audience: these are the leaders in their fields, the people who set up strategies for our future. Their words of wisdom are chosen carefully and are taken into consideration with serious global ramifications.

If I can only impress one or two of them.

This project is my baby. It's my whole world. I've invested a lot of time into this. Gave it everything I could. What if it fails? What if they don't like it? How can I convince them that it's everything I believe in? That it's something worth believing in?

It's not just me presenting tonight. The organizers of this three-day conference lined up over 20 experts, innovators, and leaders in the education field. They invited me after they learned about our project over social media. Each presenter has 20 minutes to convince the audience that their new breakthrough model is the next big thing. Will I live up to their expectations?

I'm nervous. My knees are quivering as I walk behind the stage of this elegant and huge Philadelphia Convention Center.

I can feel the sweat dripping down my back, soaking into my white button down shirt. I pull out a fabric handkerchief and wipe the sweat from my forehead, then loosen my tie.

Only five steps and two minutes separate me from the stage. It feels like an eternity. In the meantime, I stand there, controlling my breathing, clearing my dry throat, and praying that the remains of last week's hoarseness are gone. Clearing again. I have trouble focusing.

It smells like French fries in here. Why?

I am glad I went with cotton pants.

Did I remember to lock the car?

Focus.

I'm ready. I straighten my jacket as if it got wrinkled in the last five minutes.

From the wings I can see the gold letters on the big white screen announcing *"The Pencil Pro."* I can't believe it was just last night when Kenny came up with this blue and white logo. *Why is everything last minute?* I can't help but wish Kenny were here now. I release an involuntary sigh.

I rummage through my jacket's pocket once more, making sure that I didn't lose the small remote control. It's still there. Good.

Just a couple more seconds.

The lights in the auditorium dim and I hear my name called through the microphone. This is my signal.

Show time.

I jump anxiously, skipping through the five steps. My bones quiver and shake as the curtain opens.

Applause.

Standing there, in front of the silver microphone, I feel so naked, as if all my confidence has left me in the open, for everyone to see. All those opening lines of my presentation abandoned me. I stare at the logo one more time. *The Pencil Pro.*

It stares right back at me.

ഹെയ

My name is Adam Schwartz. I am an English literature and creative writing teacher at one of Maryland's most reputable high schools. I am also the CEO and founder of *The Pencil Pro*. While teaching the senior class, I often advise my students on the importance of writing a good essay for their college application.

I emphasize the point that the best way to get the college admission officer's attention is by being original and different. He or she reads dozens of application letters a day and to get them to perk up and take notice is harder than it seems.

During my tenure as a teacher, I have noticed that students—even the best and brightest among them—were often short on original ideas. And it's not just students who suffer from this impediment. Years of experience of being conformists, standing in line, and choosing the "correct" answer took its toll on me, too. Yes , I admit. It's easier to adopt existing patterns rather than coming up with my own original concepts.

The Pencil Pro is a program that empowers the brain and the person who uses it to come up with creative solutions, generating ideas and inspiring "aha" moments. *The Pencil Pro* is based on our model: "Be Empowered with Creativity," a model that aims at giving everyone the necessary tools to ignite the engine of one's brain and become empowered with creative thinking.

A few weeks ago I received a phone call asking me to present a paper describing *The Pencil Pro* at a three-day conference at the Philadelphia Convention Center. You could hear me scream "yeah!!!!" in joy. I was excited and terrified at the same time. Top innovators and leaders in the education field were invited to participate. Some 20 papers will be presented here, starting tonight. Standing in a classroom trying to teach teenagers how to develop their creativity and creative ideas is one thing, but to be standing in front of a rather large audience of accomplished adults is another altogether.

While waiting to give my presentation I couldn't stop myself from wondering how it all started....

Kenny, Drew, and I met years ago in Ms. Peters' second grade class, at the Kings Farm Elementary School. We've been close friends ever since.

In college we followed our own paths but kept in touch, and after college, we each found our way back to Maryland, not far from the Washington, D.C. border.

For Kenny, math was always a strong suit. He found pleasure in numbers. A real nerd. Not surprisingly, when it was his turn to choose a major in college, he picked analytic math and graduated Magna Cum Laude. Girls and intimate relationships were never a top priority for Kenny.

When an early-midlife crisis hit, there was no escape, not even for Kenny. When the real estate bubble burst in 2007, Kenny decided that it was his time to shine. He left his secure job at the government and found a position within a real estate investment company located in downtown D.C. He became the leader of 25 brilliant senior trade agents and had a corner office with a golden plate that stated: "Kenny Levinson, VP and Senior Trade Consultant."

Kenny changed his whole life. He pierced his ear and started riding a motorcycle.

Finally, at the age of 41 Kenny found and married the love of his life, Dylan. A year later they adopted a boy and a girl, four-year-old twins.

Now that the smile has returned to Kenny's face, even the hair that had begun to gray on his temples could not overshadow his joy.

Drew was the athlete among us. Schoolwork took third place on his priority list, right after sports and girls. In school, he was the football captain and spent all of his time at practice.

Drew had the body of a Greek god, with wide shoulders, long golden hair, and a nose complementing his dimples. Girls just adored him.

Once he graduated, Drew decided to pursue law. Since his LSAT score (Law School Admission Test) was far from the law school acceptance, he searched and found a loophole. "A suitable candidate" it said "should have strong skills and excellent abilities to lead our wrestling team." Drew applied. He was accepted and for the next few years there was no one more wounded and sore on campus than he.

In June 2001 Drew successfully passed the bar exam and found an employment opportunity with the Palmar and Cohen law firm. He took pride in his position as the immigration law counselor. In addition, twice a week, Drew volunteered to teach groups who immigrated to America after the age of 55, who had little to no English-speaking skills. The program was called the "Bilingual Citizens," but Drew called it "Group B."

He never returned to wrestling.

Drew was married twice. I attended both ceremonies. Magi, his first wife, was a beautiful social worker with dark hair and blue eyes. She was inexperienced and a virgin. They met on campus and married too young.

The marriage lasted 18 months.

His second wife, Sophia, was the complete opposite. A girl with a rich life experience who immigrated to America from Barcelona, Spain. Sophia was characterized by stormy moods, making her seem like an eternal tempest. They eloped and married in Vegas, dragging me with them to an alcohol-fueled weekend. This marriage lasted only 15 months, and many plates were slammed against the walls.

Ever since then, Drew promised to abstain from marriage. At least he's keeping his word for now.

As for me, I was the rebel of our group. In high school I had a tendency to get into trouble. I especially remember a broken window and a rope made from my mother's old clothes, hanging down as an escape route from the biology lab.

The principal's office was a place I visited quite frequently. One day, I ran into my older sister Miriam, who attended the same school as I did. As soon as I came out from the detention office, where I was waiting to receive the note releasing me from my punishment, she stood in front of me.

"The best punishment for you, little brother, is to end up as a teacher. That will teach you a lesson," she sneered.

"Over my dead body," I told her.

It turned out she was right.

Elizabeth was my last girlfriend. We lived together for a year and a half before she packed up and left, leaving no note.

Except for a teaching career and a two-bedroom apartment on 18th Street NW in D.C., I didn't have much to offer.

After so many years of friendship, Kenny, Drew, and I decided to have a night out regularly. A guy's night where we could hang at our local bar, have beer, and talk about life. We started our Thursday beer night, seven years ago, and we've tried not to ever miss it. So far, we have kept this tradition going, 9:00 p.m. at Andy's bar. Beer, guys, and complaints.

On one particular night, I was feeling saucy. Teaching and adult life had started to get to me. I've realized what was bothering me. Of course, I couldn't wait to share it with my buddies.

"You know what the problem is?" I asked as soon as I sat on the barstool. Kenny and Drew were already seated at the bar, working on their first beers. Mine was sitting on the counter, sweating as it waited for me.

"No, but I'm sure you'll tell us," Kenny commented with a grin.

"The problem is, that we all think like computers. By variables. Parameters. Black and white. Right click or left click," I said with much frustration.

"Okay, so what's the problem?" asked Drew, signaling for additional beers, though I hadn't started on mine yet.

I grabbed for the bottle. I had other things on my mind that were more important than drinking...for now.

"The problem is that we're *not* robots, we just think like them. And, by doing so, we erase our ability to engender novel ideas."

"Explain," said Kenny.

"Well," I said after swallowing my first gulp of beer, "the other week I had to visit a dermatologist. I turned on my GPS. I asked it to take me to my destination and clicked 'go.' The program asked me if I'd like to take the highway with the toll-road or without. Right? What about the other variables that I may have wanted but the program didn't ask me? What if I really wanted to go over the mountains or take the road that crosses the bridge so I could enjoy the ocean view? Or what if I have allergies and wanted to avoid the pollen from the cherry blossom trees surrounding the park because I wanted to drive with my windows down?"

"So, what's the problem? Pick any road you want. The GPS

just directs you; it doesn't order you," said Kenny signaling to the bartender to bring nachos.

"Actually, it's more than that," I said. "I love my students, and I love teaching them literature and writing, but something is bothering me. Their imagination doesn't take off. Just like us, their way of thinking is robotic in some way, almost like we are all following unwritten rules."

"So, what's your suggestion?" asked Kenny.

Somehow it was obvious that if I raised a concern, I'd have the solution or at least a general idea where to head.

They know me, maybe too well. I like to beef about it. When something irritates me, I bring it here, to our table, not far from my beer bottle. Usually, by midnight, we'll come up with a solution or at least an initiative for a change.

"So, what's your idea?" asked Kenny, bringing me back to the current concern of this century.

"It all begins with education," I declared and not for the first time. Yes, I'm one of those educators who believes that the next generation is still our chance to save the world.

"We need to change the way we think, change the way we act, create something from nothing," I explained, while the beer started to take over.

"To create something from nothing," repeated Drew, "a smart idea, like I've never heard it before," he sneered, while taking another sip from his draft beer.

I nodded saying, "Until 1959 people believed that there were only two switch modes for lights: on and off. One day a smart guy named Joel S. Spira came along and created the dimmer, right? Our brain works the same way. We need to create change. We need to cause people to think differently. Remember the GPS? What if there's more than one correct way? Remember the boy who put his finger in the dam to block the water from overflowing the city? It's exactly the same thing. This boy just thought 'out of the box' and brought his idea to the table. I'm sure there are thousands more examples like those."

"It's too late to think of that now," said Kenny as he looked at his new watch that was synchronized with his smart phone.

"Okay, fine," I said, nodding again. "But let's pretend that all of a sudden a genius steps in and suggests something that no one has thought of before. Let's say he claims that there's a parallel universe somewhere in the world and he has the key to unlock its gates. What will happen then?"

"People will make his life miserable," said Kenny.

"He'll become the joker of the media?" suggested Drew.

"Possibly true. At first, people will make an idiot out of him, a red clown with blue hair, but if he survives the public humiliation, maybe there's a chance that his idea will find its way to the starving Facebook crowd. What I mean is," I added quickly before the second bottle of beer demanded I get a cab back home, "that only a different way of thinking will bring a different solution, and we have the tools to create the next young genius."

"I say, why only young geniuses? Let's do it for all. Let's

change America!" Drew declared in a small act of patriotism.

"How exactly?" asked Kenny, whose red eyes stated that he was fantasizing of his soft pillow and blanket waiting for him at home.

"I have an idea," I said. "We should come up with exercises that ignite people's brains and lead to breakthrough ideas. We will make people understand that there are alternative ways for things they have been doing or thinking for many years. Then, people can have their own "aha" moments and be innovators if they choose. We should call it..." I looked around me, *"The Pencil Pro,"* I announced proudly and picked up a pencil that was forgotten on the bar counter.

"The Pencil Pro?" asked Drew and Kenny together.

"Yes!" I said. "PRO like in promoting original thinking." I liked the name. "Like sharpening a pencil; that's the way we can sharpen our brains and those of others in order to create a new way of thinking."

The way back home was pretty blurry.

CHAPTER 2

The next day, I woke up later than usual. On Fridays I have the day off because the school district hires retired professional teachers to cover our classes. It is compensation for a recent salary cut. The idea was to involve more professional teachers while not burdening the school's budget.

I got out of bed and washed my face. I'm not a drinker, and the beers on Thursday nights provide me with enough of a beer buzz for the entire week, so the adrenaline from last night was still pounding in my head.

I got dressed, walked into the kitchen, turned on the coffee machine, and went searching for the remote control to turn on the TV.

Another ordinary day. Nothing new. The stock market goes up, and then down again. Which reminded me, I had to run some errands before dinner with my sister, Miriam, and her husband, Rob.

I opened the half empty refrigerator to check what was missing. I searched for a piece of paper and a pencil to make my shopping list when I remembered... Pencil... Hmmm... *The Pencil Pro*.

಄಄

"Hello to the distinguished members of *The Pencil Pro*," I typed into a new group chat consisting of Kenny, Drew, Rob, and me. I've added my brother-in-law, Rob, to the group chat because I liked his artistic style and I thought it would contribute to our goals.

"Thank you for choosing to fly with us."

I added a smiley face.

"As we discussed last night, our project is being launched right now. I suggest defining our mission to create the next genius," I added in a non-serious tone.

"What did I miss?" Rob texted back.

"Hey, Rob, sorry you couldn't make it to beer night yesterday. I'll tell you all about it at dinner tonight."

"No sweat," he replied, "Lizzie and the boys are planning to put on a show for you."

"Can't wait to see the show," I texted right back and added

another smiley face. I love my niece and nephews. Lizzie will soon be five-years-old and the twins, Danny and Ben, will soon turn eight.

"Okay, back to business," I texted again in the chat, "this is how I suggest we approach it: every week we're going to come up with ideas and activities for our 'customers.' Once the activities are agreed upon, we each have 48 hours to execute the plan. At the semi-formal staff meeting that will be held on consecutive Thursday nights at 9 p.m. at Andy's Bar, we will examine our results and evaluate our success."

I ended the message in a humoristic note. "If you have any suggestions, questions, concerns, and/or comments please do not hesitate to contact me."

Two minutes later I received a text message from Drew. "So you have a day off, huh? Enjoy the freedom while you can, you're a son of a..." In Drew's language it means: I accept the plan, thanks for the message.

Kenny's was more on the practical side. "And how would we know if we've accomplished the goal?"

"Good question, Kenny," I replied, "here's my suggestion: any activity or a dilemma that receives multiple reactions that suggest different ways of solution finding will be considered a success. But any dilemmas or questions that most people reply to with the exact same solution will be considered a failure since it doesn't achieve our goal to challenge the brain. And besides, my hope is that we'll notice that the way our 'clients' think is changed or they adopted a different way of observation."

"No sweat," said Drew, "I volunteer my Group B for this experiment."

୧୦୧

It was late afternoon when I sank into the couch in my living room with the laptop on my knees. I knew how I was going to contribute to *The Pencil Pro*: I was going to give all the exercises to my students. Kenny and Drew would use their jobs, and I would use mine. Since I was aiming to find the next big genius, what better way to find him or her than in the classroom?

I needed to address the parents of my students. I knew it was my duty to send an email update to the parents regarding any changes made to the curriculum. In fact, there was no real change being made to the curriculum as it was written and approved by the county's education board. *The Pencil Pro* was simply an intention to enrich the students' points of view. The material will stay as planned, but the educational approach will be a bit different.

Nevertheless, any change, including a pedagogical one, still needed to be communicated to the students' parents. I cc'd Meredith, the principal, to back me up.

I went on to type: "My friends and I are looking for ways to turn your kids into innovators, capable of coming up with breakthrough ideas. This was an arbitrary decision that was accepted at a semi-serious board meeting at Andy's Pub, less than 24 hours ago."

My backspace key worked hard.

"Dear parents," I started again. "We all know the advantages of technology and the new methods of education that were created in order to address the needs of a modern society. I, just like you, can hardly imagine how my life would be without the benefits of advanced technology. Integrating personal computers into our educational system and expanding knowledge by taking advantage of search engines was one of the major steps necessary to be in accordance with the highest technological standards, and to be accepted in today's business world. A necessary step for our children facing the future..." Blah blah, blah...

"As a veteran teacher," I continued to write, leaving my sarcastic gibes for another day, "I'm committed to encouraging students to think and create by means of various educational methods at our disposal. During the semester, we will enrich the curriculum with original thinking exercises that will help the students develop an independent way of thinking. They will find creative solutions for ordinary, everyday issues or concerns and see the world in many colors." (The dimmer idea, remember?)

"I hope that not only will the students find interest in the exercises but also you, the parents, can participate at home. For any question or concern, please do not hesitate to contact me."

I signed my name and clicked the send button.

"*The Pencil Pro* is under way," I whispered to the screen. That's it. Now it's official. Good luck to all of us.

৪০৫৪

It was late at night, close to midnight, when I heard the incoming text message on my phone. Although I was already in bed, I couldn't fall asleep. I was over-stimulated, my mind was racing. I was making lists in my head of the things awaiting for me the following day and the pile of essays waiting to be graded on my desk.

The text message was from Drew: "I found this exercise in the newspaper. Does it fit our purpose?"

EXERCISE NO. 1

Look closely at the picture. Concentrate. Observe the small details. Clear your mind. Do not think of anything else but the picture.

Now, answer the following questions:

1. Give the picture a caption.
2. How do you think the tree feels?
3. Read the following conceptualization: "The raindrops do not bother the drowning tree." What do you think about the picture now?
4. Now turn the picture upside down. Did you change your mind?

CHAPTER 3

It was after midnight when Detective Eric Gutenheim walked toward his car, leaving the district crew behind to move in and restore the murder scene to as near normal as possible. He resisted the urge to eat, which is what he usually does when he's disturbed, and instead tried to focus on his initial impressions of what had happened at the scene. He thought of how, when he had glanced at the young beat cop who had the unfortunate task of zipping up the body bag, their eyes had met and the silent, "it's a damn shame" remark had slipped between them.

The detective grimaced beneath his bushy red mustache, making his expression even more stern than normal. He'd seen many dead people over the years. He had a Master's in criminology from NYU, but it never really prepared him for the real thing. Cold bodies. Lifeless, staring. And, while he got used to it, he never got over it: those eyes peering into the depths of your very soul, begging for understanding of the unspoken words.

He stifled the urge again and headed towards his car and yanked open the car door. Eric knew what lay ahead, a mountain of procedure and routine. The corpse, though, would be transferred to the morgue by now and, with any luck, the autopsy report would be on his desk by early afternoon. Maybe it would provide him with at least a few answers, but for some reason with this case, he very much doubted it.

As he turned the key in the ignition, his mind automatically started to evaluate the process: collecting evidence, questioning potential witnesses, gathering videos from the security cameras to check on pedestrians walking nearby, interrogating the homeless in return for a few dollars, a drink or a warm meal. A sigh escaped his bulky frame, and a stifled yawn took its chance and followed immediately afterward. Even thinking about the paperwork made him feel tired.

He hoped, as he always did, that something solid would materialize within the first 48 hours, because the trail would start to go cold after that. But, this time, his desire for good luck was a little stronger than usual; he really wanted to get the bastard who'd done this. There was something about the victim that had really shaken him, and it wasn't only that she looked much younger than the 22 years stated in her passport, which they'd found in her bag. It was the look on her face that had sent a cold chill through him. She didn't have the regular expressions of either terror or sheer surprise, but a look that seemed almost serene with her gaze fixed knowingly upon him. And her eyes weren't glazed or cloudy either, despite the fact she'd obviously been dead for some time. They were as clear and bright as if she were still living and it made him feel as if she had been trying to communicate with him.

His stomach gave an involuntary lurch as he thought of his own daughter, Missy. She was almost four years old now. She was born on the west side of Providence not long after he and Dina had moved to Rhode Island five years ago. He was a tough cop, no doubt about that, and as Station Chief he knew he would, more often than not, play a role in any of the major investigations. For Detective Eric Gutenheim the job came first. But seeing young people with their lives snatched away so suddenly and brutally had always churned his guts. Now, because of Missy, it pained him to his core.

As he steered into the darkness, Eric pulled out a plastic bag he had stuffed into the glove compartment, dug out a baby carrot, and bit into it.

ℲὉℂℜ

There was certainly enough work for Eric in the small local station, but murders and violent crime only turned up on his doorstep once or twice a year, at the most; this wasn't New York.

At the mere thought of murder, his mind slipped back to the

corpse and the waste of a young life. A pretty young girl with soft skin, big dark eyes, long black hair, and a beauty spot on her left cheek was dead. There hadn't, at least from what he saw, been any signs of a struggle. Her long-sleeve, black shirt hadn't been torn, and her blue jeans, a few sizes bigger than her tiny waist, hadn't been undone. To all intents and purposes, it seemed that someone had approached her quietly from behind, reached around her neck, and slit her throat until she was almost decapitated. When she was found, the body, the murder weapon (steel blade of a razor sharp knife), and her belongings were seemingly *deposited* almost artistically in the center of a dark pool of blood.

Next to her they'd found a small purse containing her passport, which told him that she was from the UK, that her name was Carolyn James, and that she was, had been, 22 years old. The bag also held a single lipstick, sunglasses, a key, a few bucks, and a photo ID confirming the name and giving them a mailing address, which was a P.O. box number. At least they had a good starting point. But, although it appeared to be confirmation of identity, it didn't sit well with Eric, and he just wasn't convinced.

The girl looked ethnic, not English, although he knew that didn't mean much these days, but she didn't look 22 either. If Eric had been asked to estimate her age, he would have said 16 or 17 at the most. Attached to the key they found was a small plastic tag that held a logo of the Happy Dumplings Restaurant, possibly either a place she frequented often or, more likely, her place of work, but there was something strange even about her purse. Everything was neat and normal, way too normal for his liking, considering what most women usually carried in their purses, if his wife Dina was anything to go by. That was, of course, to the exclusion of the blond wig, which they'd found in a separate paper bag close to the body. In the pocket of her jeans was found a gold necklace with a pendant. It had some weird picture of a tree engraved on it, but what seemed strange was that it was not around her neck. If it wasn't hers, then who was it for? Also, there was a strange ripped piece of paper that looked like it was torn out of an advertisement next to her on the ground. Probably for some club or something, but it looked like a flyer and had all these weird symbols on it. It was probably trash that the wind blew into the area, but Eric kept it anyway in case there was any useful DNA on it.

What on earth would a young woman, who had beautiful hair anyway, be doing with a blond wig? He tried to suppress the urge to make assumptions. They didn't even know if it actually belonged to the girl. If she had worn it though, the lab would soon let him know.

It was hard to tell yet if anything had been stolen, but, considering the contents of her bag that seemed undamaged and her undisturbed clothes, Detective Gutenheim very much doubted it.

This wasn't that kind of murder. In fact, at the moment, it didn't look like any kind of typical murder. It was too neat. The girl didn't look as if she had been scared or even surprised.

Someone had come at her from behind and gone straight for her neck with a blade. They had stolen nothing, at least that's how it appeared on the surface. She hadn't struggled or, apparently, even attempted to defend herself, because her hands had no bruises, scratches, or cuts. Even the ground around the body wasn't disturbed. She hadn't kicked, fought, or simply messed up the gravel in her death throes. She had, simply... succumbed.

Maybe, he thought, he'd get lucky and the samples taken from beneath her fingernails would shed more light on the killer's identity, but somehow he doubted it. This case was subtly different from any other he'd investigated. Different in so many ways.

Eric Gutenheim had a hunch that this investigation would not go through the familiar step-by-step "by the book" process.

He also had to concede that, while a few murders occurred during the day, most murders happened at night when the streets are empty and dark. Yet, it certainly looked like this one had taken place sometime in the afternoon. The post-mortem would confirm his suspicions.

On top of that, bodies were usually found in their own homes, in parks, or behind trash bins in dark alleys. This one had been found under the Indian Point Park Bridge with no sign of having been taken there after the murder. The pool of blood surrounding the body told him that she had been killed in situ. The girl, the deceased, Carolyn, had gone there of her own free will and been taken down. Taken down without a struggle, without apparently defending herself, dying with a look of...Eric struggled to find the right word...contentment. Yes, that was it. The girl had died with a look of contentment on her face.

That was another thing, what the hell was she doing there in the first place? That old bridge track led to nowhere. In fact, the only people who used it were the down-and-outs who tended to go there when it was raining. It hadn't been raining today. Had she been deliberately taken there? Maybe at gunpoint? Or had she gone of her own free will with someone she knew? But, if she had, why would she then turn her back on someone and stand passively while they cut her throat? Or had she simply been passing by; ending up to be the unlucky one the killer had been hoping for? If that was the case though, he was back to square one. Where had she been going?

He bit into another baby carrot and looked down at it in disgust. The baby carrots weren't really good, but how could he say no to Dina? After all, with another child on the way, it made sense that she wanted him as healthy as could be, and even he had to admit his 6'3" frame had been looking a lot more stocky in recent years. Another sigh escaped him. He pushed thoughts of his family and impending middle age from his mind, trying instead to refocus on the job at hand.

What about motive? The most popular reasons for murder are money, revenge, or betrayal, but there were others, of course. Murdering someone over drugs or to protect secrets often came high on the list. But Eric was having a hard time believing this particular murder involved any of the usual reasons. Prostitutes are also often seen as being easy victims but, if this girl was a prostitute—and it might tie in with why she was under the bridge in the first placeshe certainly didn't look like one. Neither did it look as if she had been sexually assaulted. Although she wasn't carrying a lot of money, she did have some. If it was a *John* looking for a refund, then her money would have been gone for sure. If it was a psycho on a mission from God, then it was certainly the neatest maniacal attack he'd even seen.

He took another bite of a baby carrot and threw the rest out of the window. The rats wouldn't go hungry, and Dina never needed to know.

CHAPTER 4

From the darkest mind of a potential killer:

Blood. It was everywhere. Accursed blood decorates the world. Dripping from the mouth and blurring the pupils. Painting the walls red.

And the smell? So strong in the air. Invading the nostrils, burning the throat.

A smell of scorched metal. The smell of death. It's not me. I am innocent.

I was innocent.

I've done nothing wrong. I swear on my life. They brought me here. Forced me. They persecute me during nights. They hunt me during the days.

And the sleep? Nightmares. I scream, I kick. I resist. Awaken in a cold sweat. Help me! Have mercy! I beg...

It's so cold in here, and dark. The bright moon is beyond reach and the stars are mocking me. The metal handcuffs are freezing cold. They chafe my ankles and slash at my cold dead soul.

I want to be free. To run for my life. To wander to infinity with no boundaries, but I am not alone.

Don't judge me. Let me explain. Let me convince you that I am innocent. It's not my fault.

It's theirs. It's the family you were born in, binding you in chains, commanding you with guilt.

Help me! Don't force me to slaughter. I simply cannot....

Who am I? What am I? What have I become? I'm that person. The person who walks beside you in the street. The one who stands next to your door.

Let me tell you my story.

CHAPTER 5

"Are you kidding me?" Rob replied in the group chat, referring to the drowning tree exercise. "You know what happens to a tree of this kind and at this age when it is drowning in a flood? It is doubtful whether it will be possible to save it and dry out its trunk. It's completely rotten. Even trees that survive the flood will be vulnerable. They are exposed to diseases and other natural disasters. It is a lost tree and impossible to create anything from it."

I could guess that the first exercise irritated my brother-in-law. Rob, a very talented guy, worked as a data analyst for a few years but was soon fed up with the long, demanding hours and frequent travel requirements. When the kids were born, Miriam and Rob decided that Miriam should keep her position as a veterinarian and the owner of the pet clinic, and Rob would quit his job and focus on his role as stay-at-home dad.

Rob was blessed with golden hands, so home improvements were done by him. He even planned the addition of another bedroom and bathroom. His spare time was dedicated to his studio and passion for woodcarving. The big lamp hanging from my living room ceiling was his creation.

"Interesting perspective," Drew replied. "I'm waiting for my meeting with Group B tonight to hear what they think."

"My guys were headed in the same direction as Rob," wrote Kenny, "my team has the brightest minds! They immediately assumed that this tree is in a disaster-stricken area, and quoted data citing the rate risk for investment in areas prone to flooding. It is interesting that this picture led us into a discussion of whether to increase the related insurance purchasing group attached to purchase property in areas struck by disaster."

"I wonder what the kids' reactions were?" Drew asked.

"Not yet," I replied, "my 9th grade class begins in an hour. I'll keep you posted tonight."

"Yes, me too. I'll text again once we end the Group B session. Have to run. The boss is waiting," Drew wrote.

80Q3

"An interesting image." Alex smiled. Alex was the expert photography student in my class. He examined the image from multiple angles, blocking half of it with his fist, and then exposing some of it to the sun and shadow. He was fascinated. You could see the wheels turning in his head. Photography was his world.

"I'm more curious with the sentence written under the picture," Anne admitted. "Here, listen: 'Even big drops of water do not interfere with the drowning tree,'" she changed it slightly. "It feels to me as if the tree has been apathetic to what is happening. Lost cause, the poor tree has given up. He knows that he's going to die no matter what happens now."

"Yes, it reminds me of a man at an office with a flood of work that no matter how much more shit is thrown at him," said Mark, "he is helpless. He'll never come out of the mud."

"What do you think, Jen?" I asked. Jen is a bright student and a quiet one. She always has an interesting perspective related to the philosophy of life. Jen is quick to debate issues such as who the object in question is and what ethical and moral dilemma it carries. If I do not approach her and "drag" her into the discussion, she will choose to be a bystander.

"I...don't really know," she hesitated.

"How does it feel to you, Jen? This situation. Do you see anything else in here?"

"I," she hesitated again, paused for a moment then said, "I think if I had to give a name to this picture, I would call it a dialogue between life and death."

"Why?" I insisted.

"Because, on the one hand, this rain is what trees and every living creature need in order to survive. Right? On the other hand, it is sinking in the wet mud, the fear that the land will cover you, swallow you in, before you..." She paused.

"Before what?" I refused to let her off the hook.

"I don't know, before you have enough time to adjust to the change, save yourself, find a way to keep and straighten the top of your head above the mud."

"OK, friends," I added, "now, try to turn the picture upside down. Do you see anything else in here?"

Their eyes lit up at once. I saw a mix of puzzled looks with hesitation. How did we miss it? What does it mean?

Silence in the classroom.

"Okay," I took control again, "anyone else want to comment on the photo?" According to the silence I understood that this topic is done and covered.

"Let's move on. Open your books to page 43."

⅋℈

It was almost midnight when Drew sent a voice message to our group chat.

"I'm exhausted. Dying to go to bed. A long day at the office and a maniac judge scheduled a hearing at 8:00 a.m. So here's a quick report from Group B. If you want more details, 1 will elaborate tomorrow. It turns out that my students believe there is a token, or a kind of parable that is hidden behind the picture.

They talked about differences in perceptions of the 'tree' as a symbol between foreign cultures. However, all agreed that you must respect the trees no matter what culture you come from.

"In the Chinese culture, for example, the tree symbolizes the connection between life and death, between heaven and earth, and between matter and spirit. The blossoms symbolize wisdom and knowledge; the trunks symbolize strength and security; the sturdy roots represent stability and longevity. Fruit symbolizes the next generation, bark symbolizes human protection from disease, and green leaves are a symbol for life and immortality. Thus, in their view, the symbolism of the drowning tree is the sinking of dreams, knowledge, wisdom, and the sinking of the next generation and fulfillment. Definitely not a good thing."

"I agree," Kenny wrote. "In Judaism we say: a man is like a tree of the field, which means the tree has a soul just like a human being."

"Of course," Rob responded, "and people who believe that the tree brings good luck will knock on wood three times to keep away bad luck."

"Wait! I'm not done," Drew sent another voice message. "And what are you doing up so late? Basically, people who emigrated from Africa told us that some tribes believe that spirits are hiding in the trees, and therefore, cutting down a tree is considered not only an attack on nature but mainly it is harm done to the soul. A man who cuts down a tree brings bad luck upon himself, as well as physical and property damage. The older and more mature the tree is, the more harm he will cause and the more damage he will commit. Okay. I'm done now."

There was a moment of silence in the group chat before Kenny responded.

"I have an idea for our next exercise," Kenny texted. "I think the next exercise will suit all of us, and it is also something I wanted to do a long time ago. I will send you the details in the morning."

EXERCISE No. 2

This exercise is called "A closed book is nothing but a stack of paper."

Take a thick book and lay it on the table.

1. What do you think can be done with the book other than read it?
2. Start with the end. Read the last paragraph in the book and try to guess: "What was in the story?"

ଛୀଓ୫

Kenny thought about this exercise for a long time. He knew exactly what the purpose was and how it should be displayed in the next team meeting. He will ask the agents to read the last page of the annual data report to be published next week. He was always curious to know whether it is possible to guess the market trends just by the last page of the annual summary data. But more than that, he was curious to know if his veteran real estate agents could not only analyze the market trends, according to the data in their possession, but also predict future market trends.

Rob decided to try this exercise on his children. On Tuesday night, after helping them bathe and get ready for bed, he had a surprise in store for them.

"Dad has a surprise for us, Dad has a surprise," little Lizzie rejoiced as her two older twin brothers, Ben and Danny, soon approached, mesmerized by the brightly wrapped package in Rob's hands.

"What is it, Dad? What's the surprise?" They were curious.

"First brush your teeth and put on your pajamas." Within a few minutes, the kiddies were ready.

That morning, following the introduction of the second exercise of the program, Rob rushed to the bookstore to buy a new children's book. The book's title was *Once Upon a Time In a Place Far, Far Away.* He trusted his kid's imagination.

"Let's get started," said Rob. "First, look at this book," he held the closed book, lying in the palm of his right hand. "What do you see?"

"A book?" Ben was also confused.

"A new book for kids," said Danny examining the details.

"Read it, Daddy," exclaimed Lizzie. "A new book." She clapped her hands.

"Okay, don't worry, soon enough we'll read the book, but before we do, can you tell me what else we can do with this book, just as it is now, closed."

"Maybe press a flower between its pages?" Ben suggested hesitantly. He remembered they used to do it in the spring sometimes.

"Nice idea," said Rob. "True, we could dry a flower between its pages. What else?"

"You can place it on the floor and climb on it to reach the cookie jar," Lizzie suggested. The boys laughed.

"True, my little smarty pants," Rob kissed her on the cheek. "You can use it as a small stool. What else?"

"You can squash mosquitoes on to the walls," Danny said. The four of them laughed.

"You can cut the pictures from the book with scissors and make one big picture," Lizzie said, her face glowing with the idea of a new art project.

"True," Rob agreed. "It is called a collage."

"I actually was thinking..." Danny hesitated.

"What, honey?" Rob patted Danny's head, encouraging him to continue.

"I was thinking that anything can be actually used for something else..." Danny paused.

"How's that?" asked Rob gently.

"Here." Danny pointed to the Lizzie's pink hula hoop. "You know how many things we can do with that?"

"Like...?" Rob asked

"You can use it as a giant key ring, or flying disc, or yo-yo, or even as a giant cookie cutter."

"He's right!" Ben was excited. "Daddy, do you know how many things you can do if you melt a Lego block? You can make so many shapes out of that or even use it as a glue."

Rob was silent for a while. How come he, with all of his experience as a woodcarving artist, never thought of that? He knew that kids have a better imagination than adults, yet he couldn't stop wondering what happened to our imaginations. Was it just a coincidence or did we all lose our imaginations somewhere along the way?

"Now can you read us the story?" asked Lizzie, yawning.

"Of course," Rob replied, "but let's do something different, okay?"

"Something different?" the kids repeated, looking at each other quizzically.

"Okay, so now I'm going to read to you the last page of the book and you have to tell me what you think happened before, okay?"

The kids were obviously disappointed. "So you're just going to read the last page?"

"Yes. Today I will only read the last page, and I'll let you guess what happened in the story, but tomorrow I promise to read the whole story. Okay?"

The children nodded. "Okay, Daddy."

"So, here it goes. Listen," said Rob while he flipped to the last page and read:

"It was late at night and the moon was glowing in the sky.

'It's time to go to bed,' Mom whispered gently, holding Michael's hand. Mom's hand was soft and warm like a blanket.

Michael was very tired and yawned.

It was a long day. A happy and a sad day. Full of adventures.

They found magical places and met kind and good-hearted people.

The world is round and beautiful, they knew, but now it is the time to go home.

Good night."

When he was done, Rob closed the book and laid it beside him.

"So, what do you think?" He looked at their eyes and saw their confusion. "What happened before Michael and his mom went back home?"

"I think they went for a walk," Lizzie proposed. "Maybe they got lost."

"Yes," Ben seemed excited, "and they probably traveled to many mysterious places and flew in the sky with a magic blanket."

"And they met a pink fairy who gave them a magic goodnight

kiss," Lizzie whispered as she closed her eyes.

"I actually think that Michael was lost and the mother went to look for him," Danny suggested, "and good people gave them food and water and a home and a cell phone so they can call home. And you said that they understood that the world is round, right? So for sure Michael tried to go to the end of the world and see if Earth is round or flat."

Rob smiled. "That's a possibility."

"So what was it? What's the correct answer?" Ben asked. "How do we know what really happened in the story? Who's right?"

"Everyone is right tonight," Rob told the children. "There is no right or wrong answer to imagination. Imagination has no limits or boundaries. Tomorrow we'll know what the writer chose to tell us. Remember, stories are endless."

"Oh no," Ben said, "I wanted to find out now."

"There isn't always a definite answer, son." Rob tousled Ben's hair playfully.

"Read us the story, Daddy. Please?" Lizzie asked, yawning again.

"Tomorrow, my princess, I promise. I'll read it tomorrow, and now good night. Sweet, sweet dreams."

Rob kissed each one of them and left the room.

No doubt kids have the best imagination. Rob smiled. He couldn't point out the exact thing that made this exercise successful or why it encouraged greater imagination and expression in children. However, as far as Rob was concerned, exercise number two was a winner.

CHAPTER 6

The pathology report landed on Detective Gutenheim's desk just after lunch the next day. He flipped through the pages and sighed until he reached the last page that determined cause of death: excessive blood loss.

No evidence of drug use was found in the body.

The lab also sent back a separate report on the golden necklace with the pedant, and the ripped piece of paper found in the victim's jean's pocket. The lab could not find any evidence for DNA except for the victim's fingerprints.

Yet something else caught his eye and caused Eric to close the bright yellow file, slowly, before placing it neatly on his desk by the side of the official fax he'd received that morning from the US Department of Homeland Security. The fax included the victim's fingerprints and photo, which were both taken at the US Customs and Border control when she entered the country at

JFK Airport in New York.

There could be no question that the information corresponded with the British passport she was carrying in the name of Carolyn James, but Eric, or rather the path lab, had found another inconsistency. Although her passport stated that she was 22 years old, the pathology report claimed that, based on the minimal fusing of her bone structure, she was actually no more than 18 years old, which would also tie in with Eric's immediate impressions that she was around 16, maybe 17. According to the fax, she'd flown in to the US alone, approximately six months ago and carried only a tourist visa.

Eric felt as if Carolyn James might not be her real name.

Fake age, fake name, and fake passport?

He reached for the first drawer in his desk and pulled out a pad of yellow sticky notes.

On the first note he wrote: *Forged passport.*

On the second note he wrote: *Victim's height: 5'2"*

On the third note he wrote: *Victim's weight: 115 pounds.*

On the next sticky note he wrote the estimate time of death: *Tuesday, November 15, between 1:20 p.m. and 3:00 p.m.*

The sticky notes began to spread across the top of his desk.

The blond wig found next to the body had been determined by the lab to have been used by the deceased. Gutenheim's next sticky note asked the question:

Wig. Why?

On the next sticky note he wrote: *The Happy Dumpling.*

The next sticky notes said: *No home address*? He copied the P.O. box number that was found on her ID card.

"Are you keeping a secret?" Eric whispered to the smiling face in the photo. "Let's see if we can't uncover it, shall we?"

There was a knock on the door, jolting him from his thoughts.

"Eric?" The bald head of George, the front desk officer, peered around the door.

"What can I do for you, George?" Eric asked still staring down at the photograph.

"There's someone out front who wants to speak to you, sir."

Eric gave him a questioning look but said nothing before standing and following him through the door.

The waiting room was small and painted in smoky white, which had slightly yellowed over the years. A few wooden benches with black metal legs stood against one wall, and a single table covered with colorful magazines was bolted to the floor as if to serve as a reminder as to where they really were.

George pointed silently to a little girl sitting quietly next to an old Asian-looking woman. Both looked nervous as they held each other's hand tightly.

As Eric approached them, he guessed that the girl was around the same age as his daughter, Missy, somewhere around three and not more than four years old. He kneeled next to her to be the same height as the girl, then held out his hand toward the child.

"I'm Detective Gutenheim. How can I help you?" he asked in a soft voice.

His attempts at reducing their nervousness didn't work; Eric could see fear flash in the girl's eyes as she pushed her blonde hair out of her eyes and clung to the old woman before burying her face in her lap. Eric looked questioningly at the woman and saw fear in her eyes, maybe a little despair, too.

"Sir.... Please.... Maybe.... You can help us?" the old woman queried.

Eric wondered who this couple was. His first guess was that the woman was her babysitter, but for some reason, she seemed a little reluctant to clarify the reason for their visit to the police station.

Suddenly, the girl's fear burst from her into the sound of sobbing. Eric's instinct was to reach out to stroke the child's hair. His hand was lightly touching the back of her hair when he froze. The blonde hair was no more than a synthetic blonde wig.

"Mommy," the girl choked through the sobs, "I want my mommy...."

"Please sir..." said the old Asian woman, "please... take this..." She handed him a crumbled piece of paper.

"What is it?" asked the detective.

"It's ... address ... for the girl."

Eric opened the note carefully. In black ink was written: 23 Hope St. Apartment 202. Suddenly he was jolted back into cop mode.

He looked up at the woman, "Do you have a name, ma'am?"

"Yes, sir. I am Qi Liang."

"Are you related to this child?"

"No, sir. I'm the babysitter. Night-time."

"Why?" asked Eric.

"The other girl, the mother, she works at my family's restaurant to clean."

"The mother?"

"Yes, sir. She work very hard. Quiet girl. Nice. No trouble."

"But she didn't come back today, right?" Eric hazarded.

"No, sir. And now I not know what I do."

"Is the name of your family restaurant The Happy Dumpling?" Eric asked with a burst of fire in his voice.

"Yes, sir," the old woman replied.

Eric looked at the child again and stared hard. Are there any other kids who are waiting at that apartment, he wondered, maybe a third person? Maybe a father.

Now, at least, Eric had her home address written on the note.

It turned out that the babysitter didn't really know much about the two girls. In fact, from what he could understand, Carolyn, if that was her real name, hardly spoke English, which seemed a little odd for a woman who was supposedly Anglo-Saxon to start with. It would also contrast with the child who, from what Eric could see, spoke English as well as you could expect from any three year old. He had at least learned the little girl's name, Louisa, according to the old Chinese woman. It seemed, he decided, the old woman was telling the truth, or at least what she believed to be the truth. But Eric knew that his gut instinct had been right from the start. This wasn't going to be a run-of-the-mill case.

ᔓᔕ

The screaming tires cut the air as the wheels of Gutenheim's car screeched to a halt at the curb next to 23 Hope Street, with the backup car following close behind.

Eric's head was starting to feel fit to burst particularly as he'd had very little sleep. They had a dead girl wearing a blond wig and likely carrying a false passport, and now her alleged child showed up at the station doorstep.

Eric was barking orders as he and the other officers raced toward the stairs. "Check that the key we found in her bag matches the lock," he instructed one of the officers. "Turn the place upside down but make sure you don't destroy any evidence."

Oh, good, the forensic mobile lab is coming, too , thought Eric. "Let's see if they can find any fingerprints that match any criminals in the system."

As instructed, the officer turned the key in the lock and the door clicked open.

"It's a match, sir."

Eric stepped inside alone, and his men waited quietly behind while he surveyed the scene.

The apartment had hardly any furniture. It was a single room divided in two with a green cloth curtain hanging from the ceiling. Bare walls, two mattresses rolled on the floor, two pillows, and one blanket. A small wooden chest and a small desk with two chairs. One large fan stood in one corner of the room. There was, in truth, little to search. In another corner were two faded brown suitcases that contained some clothes, some women's underwear, and white shirts for a small girl.

Along one wall, there was a sink and counter top with a hot plate, one large pot for cooking, and an old electric kettle. Some chipped plates, soup bowls, and a few pieces of silverware had been left in the sink.

Off the large room was a small bathroom with a toilet and an improvised shower that almost looked like a garden hose hanging out of the wall behind a pinned-up plastic table cloth. Behind a chair next to the bed was a large blue bucket and red washtub that was likely used for laundry.

Some old broken toys were scattered about the room, and almost without thinking, Eric bent down and picked up a rag doll from the floor. It was worn, sticky, and "well loved" by a child's heart.

Eric could not help but compare it to the palace of dolls adorning his Missy's room.

But what was missing here? Which part of the big picture couldn't he see?

He indicated to his officers to enter, and it wasn't long before one of them yelled at him.

"Sir, look at this!" an officer shouted.

"What is it?"

The officer pointed to a heavy, black hardcover book lying under the wooden chest, in the space between the bottom drawer and the floor.

Eric pulled a disposable glove from an inside pocket, put it on his right hand and raised the thick book. Eric assumed that it had not been used for some time as the spine of the book looked somewhat new. He opened the cover but didn't see any name or its owner's address as he hoped he would. He didn't understand the writing in the book, but after a few moments he realized the book was written in Arabic. Was it Carolyn's? Was it randomly forgotten by the previous tenants?

A few things began to make sense to Eric. If Carolyn didn't speak English, then she must speak Arabic. It also made sense that the passport was fake. She wasn't English, but rather, from a Middle Eastern or Arabic country. Eric continued to mull over the book.

"The book should be read backwards," offered one of the police officers. "Since it's in Arabic, you should probably open and read it from the back cover to the front, like reading from the end to the beginning," he explained.

Eric flipped the book to the other side and saw what appeared to be a title page and copyright information. He began to scan the pages for some sort of signature or name written inside, but he found nothing. He didn't know how to read Arabic. On the last page, under the Arabic letters, was written something in English in a pencil. He squinted his eyes. Eric read out loud: **"There is more to it than meets the eye."**

"It's the Koran," another officer offered. "It's the sacred Muslim book."

Eric nodded. "Give it to the forensics to check it for fingerprints, and keep looking through this place thoroughly, please," he ordered.

"Good job, Steve." He patted the officer who found the book on his shoulder.

From the corner of his eye, he saw that the forensics mobile lab detectives were running some data in their computer.

"Anything?" he said hopefully.

"No, nothing so far," Susan replied. She was the head of the Fingerprints and DNA mobile lab. "Standard fingerprints. We're running some data in the computer but so far no match to our criminal records. We'll need a couple more hours to finish our search here, but you know, it's only the initial search. I'll keep you posted if we learn anything more, Eric."

"Thanks," he replied.

Eric looked around the apartment as the men combed their way through it. Who was Carolyn? What was her real name? Did she run away from someone? Why is there no record prior to her arrival at JFK airport? The only Carolyn James who carried the same passport identification number in the official state records died in 1925 from dysentery. There was no record of a daughter entering the States. So, she was either smuggled in, brought in on a fake passport, or she was born in the US, which certainly didn't tally with the date Carolyn was supposed to have arrived.

He scratched his head and wondered just how complicated this case could get. The deeper they got into it, the more questions arose and fewer answers appeared.

"Okay," he said, almost to himself. "Let's go back down and talk to the landlord."

Two officers were holding the landlord in the hallway. The officers were extensively questioning him. The guy was a young Asian, sloppily dressed and shaking like a leaf. He didn't seem pleased to encounter Eric's company.

"Did you rent her this place?" Eric asked.

"Y-y-es, s-si-r-r," the guy stuttered. "This is not my apartment... I mean it is mine now...It belonged to my parents, but... they died a long time ago... many years ago ... in the hospital."

"What's your name?"

"Chung Lu, sir."

"How well did you know her, your tenant?"

"Not at all, s-s-sir, s-sorry, sir-r... I only saw her once. I gave her the key. I live downstairs. I just got an envelope un-under my doormat once a month with cash... $600 ... all-always on time... never late. That's all I know... no papers, no rental agreement, just cash, nothing more, sorry, s-sir."

"How did she find the place?"

"I don't know, sir. I posted some notes in a few restaurants in the area. I think maybe someone told her about it... She ... she came to me, sir. Gave me cash... put it in my hands. I gave her the keys. That's all... sorry, sir..."

"Keys? We only found one key. Was there anyone else living in the apartment, other than the girl and her daughter?"

"I don't know, sir. I never saw anyone. Just the young woman and the child. I saw them only one time. I know nothing. Really... I'm sorry."

Eric sighed. There was nothing more he wanted to pursue at this juncture.

"Okay, here's my card. If you do remember anything, give me a call. Understood?"

"Yes, s-sir-r, sure, sir... sorry, sir... I know nothing."

Eric leaned against the door, mulling over the facts in his mind as his officers continued to search the apartment.

A little girl comes to a foreign country. She must wear a wig and hide. Broken toys, no friends, and only one miserable rag doll. He rolled it over in his mind over and over again. Why? Did they feel that they had to wear wigs? Who are they hiding from? What kind of danger are they in that they had to sneak into the country? Are they in danger? Were they in danger? Why didn't they come to the police to ask for help? And now there's an orphaned girl, a child without a mother who might be in danger herself.

ഇരു

Back at the station, Eric let the old Chinese woman stay until Sydney, from Child Welfare and Protective Services, came to the station.

Eric knew the child would be protected in the safe hands of Sydney. She had been working at Child Welfare for nearly 30 years and was nicknamed "The Grandma." She was supposed to retire years ago but had refused, and no one dared to argue with her. Besides, if she wanted to stay and continue to care for children, who were they to disagree because, no doubt about it, Sydney was the best in the business. Eric had worked with her on several occasions and knew she was a kind, but extraordinarily practical woman, who loved kids with all her heart. Sydney was always ready to help, no matter what the time of day or the week.

"How are you, Eric?" Sydney asked when she entered his office.

"Hey, Syd. What do you think of Louisa?" he asked.

"Sweet kid. Unbelievably frightened, which is to be expected. She's in the other room playing with her babysitter. George is keeping an eye on them."

He shook his head. "It's a strange one, Sydney. We have one murdered girl and, it would seem, a daughter who was left behind with a neighbour. No one else in sight, and the girl is asking for her mom," he said, shaking his head again. "I don't know, Sydney. There are so many things about this case that simply don't add up. So many things are hidden and so much more to be revealed. At the moment though, my concern is for the child and not simply because Mom isn't coming back. If there is a murderer out there targeting this family, then this child has to be kept, not only calm, but also safe."

His final comments, Sydney knew, were not a statement but a question.

"She'll be fine with us, Eric. Can you make sure, though, that we have some officer cover? We are hoping to arrange a foster family at least for the moment. Much better than sending her off to some institutional care home."

He smiled. "Sure. I've been rearranging duty rosters while I waited for you."

They exchanged understanding glances but said nothing before Sydney went off to the other room to see Louisa again. Then, Eric made the call he really didn't want to.

Elaine Hernandez was Eric's protégé, and he was her mentor. She was a senior police investigator who stood at a skinny 4'9", in her early 30s with long black hair and dark blue eyes. She was a bright young woman with a sharp intellect who was never afraid to challenge Eric.

She was tough, also on a well-earned leave, and Eric was reluctant to make her break it. Still, he needed a second pair of eyes in this case, and he knew that Elaine wouldn't kick up a fuss because she never did.

୨୦୯ଌ

It was early Monday morning when Eric made the follow-up call. Although he had a nice weekend with his family, which was exceptional for him, given that his job demanded that he'd be on call 24/7, he couldn't stop thinking of Louisa.

"I'm just calling to see how Louisa is doing," he said as soon as Sydney answered.

"It's hard, Eric." Sydney sighed. "She's a young girl, still wakes up in the middle of the night and cries for her mom. We found her a great foster family, Jackie and her husband, Aaron Johnson. They are a lovely couple with five grandchildren and two cats. But it's still hard for Louisa. She needs more time, much more time."

"Of course. I understand. As much time as she needs," Eric said. "Tell me something," he added, "were you able to ask her if she remembers anything?"

"Hardly, Eric. She is very young. She doesn't remember anything. We tried, but nothing came out. The Chinese babysitter came to visit Louisa last night. Louisa was happy to see her, and they played for a long time. She told us that she used to babysit Louisa every night when the mother was working until she came home in the morning. Can you imagine, Eric? A young girl who needs to go out and clean restaurants to support her child?

"Sometimes, the mother asked the babysitter to come babysit Louisa earlier when she needed to do some shopping or run some errands. The same day the mother disappeared, she asked her to come early, around noon, because she had some things to take care of, but she never came back."

"That's interesting," Eric noted. "Things to take care of? And what were those things?"

"She didn't say. All we managed to get out was that when the mother didn't return by her usual time the following morning she began to worry. That's how they ended up at the police station. Poor girl," Sydney sighed. "She still hopes that her mother was lost, and someone can find her and bring her home."

"Has it ever happened before?" Eric asked. "I mean, her mom left the house early and came back after a while?"

"We don't really know. The old woman says no, and Louisa doesn't remember. She doesn't even know where she was born. The mother has never talked about her family or of any relatives. She only remembers that she was brought into the apartment at night because everything was dark. There was a lot of noise and screaming. Maybe she was even blindfolded. Suddenly she felt her mom's arms holding her and singing a song so she wouldn't be afraid. Maybe it was just a dream."

"Well, maybe I can help out a little because I have something for her," Eric said, glancing down at his office desk and seeing the dirty old rag doll that he found at the victim's apartment the other day. This, he felt sure, would be the child's favorite toy. "I'll drop it off on the way home, okay?"

"Of course, Eric. I'm sure Louisa will be happy. She already went out to play, but I'm happy to pass it to her. See you soon then."

Although he felt guilty for leaving the case file with one of his colleagues that night, when Eric arrived home, he rushed to kiss and hug Dina. Then he bent down and kissed her belly.

"Is everything okay?" she whispered softly in his ear.

Eric always tried to draw a sharp line between his work and family life. Rarely did he let his frustration from work affect his personal life, no matter how bad he felt.

"Yes," he muttered. "Everything is all right. I've just missed you today." He knew that if he shared the recent investigation with Dina, it would only upset her, and given her condition, that was the last thing he wanted.

He walked to his room and changed into comfortable clothes before washing his face with cold water. The cool water refreshed him. From there he went straight to Missy's room. Missy was busy playing with her dollhouse and didn't even notice his presence.

She laid the doll with the gold hair on the top floor of the dollhouse and whispered, "You are my princess. Your dreams are my dreams." Then she kissed the doll and placed another doll next to the princess. "You will be her prince," she whispered.

On the lower floor of the dollhouse she placed a small furry teddy bear. "You are their child. Play nicely and do not make too much noise. Soon Mommy and Daddy will bring you a surprise from the hospital, yes, another baby to play with, but you have to be patient, okay?" She kissed the teddy bear tenderly.

Eric could not hold back any longer. He approached his princess, picked her up, and held her in his arms. He held her close to his heart. "You are my princess," he whispered and kissed her nose.

Missy clung to him tightly, enjoying his warmth. "Daddy," she laughed and hugged his neck.

"Your dreams are..." he let her finish the sentence.

"Are my dreams," she laughed.

He kissed her again and again on her cheeks and forehead.

Kids have those game codes that adults would never understand, thought Eric. What makes them laugh may not work with our logic. It's like a completely different world of cryptograph, an internal world of imagination. Eric was jealous. He missed those days.

"Dinner is ready," Dina called from the dining room.

Eric carried Missy to the table as if she were a plane. She laughed with delight, and the sound filled the house.

CHAPTER 7

The following Monday morning I was walking to class all excited and ready. I was holding a piece of paper with a story I wrote the night before.

I'm not a professional writer, not even close to becoming one, but I do find pleasure in writing short stories. Until now, I never shared any of my writing with anyone.

I really hoped that the students would like it, and more important than that, I hoped the short story I was about to read to them would encourage them to think.

It was also the first time I shared something I wrote with my friends.

"Come on, that's a killer!" Drew was enthusiastic over the exercise in the text message. "I have no idea what the hell is written here, but the story is hot, bro!"

"I agree," said Kenny and added a smiley face.

"Where is it from?" Rob was curious to know.

"I confess. I wrote it myself. Just felt like it."

"Cool idea, amigo."

"Thanks, Drew. Goodnight."

⃝⃝

"Good morning," I said as I walked into my first-period class, which was made up of mostly sophomores.

"Good morning." The students turned toward me drowsily. Well, it was Monday morning, 7:44 a.m. I didn't expect too much.

"How was the weekend?" I always ask on Mondays, giving students some time to wake up.

"Not enough time to sleep," said Benji.

"Why?" I smiled.

He sprawled on the table.

"Scout camping trip," he muttered. "No sleep for two nights and only four hours last night." He rubbed his eyes and threatened to swallow us all with his yawn.

"Go to sleep earlier today," I offered.

"You mean right now?" He put his head back on the table.

"Well, let's do something else today," I suggested, which seemed to spark some interest.

"I'll read you a short story. Then I'll ask you to find a partner to work with. I'll give you 10 minutes to decode the flash card attached to the story. Deal?"

"Deal," everyone agreed.

"Here it goes," I said. I opened the folded paper and began to read.

Exercise No. 3

Read the following story and convert the coded message into words at the end of the exercise.

The train engine whistled, and a smell of burnt rubber filled the air as the train pulled into the station. Time to go. I coughed as I pushed and continued to make my way through the hundreds of people who hurried toward the platform. I must catch that train. No other way!

The station was smelly, a mix of scorched metal and beggars who had not showered in days. Sweat that clung to the cloth, and big ceiling fans that were expected to circulate the air but just made heavy noise and nothing else.

I kept pushing my way. My muscles ached carrying the heavy suitcase. It must weight 40 or 50 pounds. I refused to give up. This is the last train for tonight, and I'll be dammed if I let it go without me. I must find my seat, but where the hell is car G8?

Oh, yeah! Here it is! Good. I climbed the stairs and pulled up the suitcase behind me. The seats were covered in blue velvet cloth that had seen better days. Well, who cares? I lowered the backpack from my shoulder and threw a curse into the air.

She came toward me. "Take it," she said. Her big black eyes appeared frightened. I felt a folded cardboard shoved into my hand. I didn't have time to respond.

"They're chasing me," she whispered. Her eyes rolled from side to side. Gypsy. Black headscarf and wispy white hair. She wore a black dress, with large pink flowers, that was dirty and muddy. She smelled of sweet-sour sweat. Footsteps were heard. She shuddered. "I must go now," she whispered, "before they get me." She disappeared as if she were nothing more than a puff of air. I felt the piece of cardboard in my hand.

Another long whistle and the train started to move. I took a deep breath of relief. I made it. I'm here. On the way out from this middle-age neglected town. Now everything should be fine.

But what was I supposed to do with this note now?

෪෨

Half an hour later I had lots of ideas for deciphering the code card. I looked at the students' interpretations that were written on flash cards and were gathered into a pile. I was a bit shocked, I must admit. Each card had a different idea. No repeats. Each pair of students interpreted the code in a different way.

"Okay, so what's the right answer?" one of the students asked curiously.

"Uh," I cleared my voice, "I don't really know."

"What? That's weird. What do you mean you don't know? You mean there's no answer? We worked for nothing? So, what do those card codes mean?"

"That's exactly it. There is no real meaning to the card. Anyone can come up with their own interpretation."

The students fell silent. "So, that's it? The story has no ending?" They were baffled. They are all used to getting a clear-cut answer, or at least some kind of feedback if their ideas are on the right track.

"What now?" someone asked.

"Before we move on, I have to plant an idea in your minds related to this exercise. Take the time to reflect. I do not expect you to share with me your thoughts right away. Okay? What happens if I change the situation? In other words, let's say I tell you that the teacher gives Jose a folded note and says, 'Can you please give it to your mother? She'll understand what's written on the note.' Will you decipher the same code that you just worked on in the same way?"

I looked around me. An ominous silence seemed to envelop the class, but their eyes were shining.

"Okay, let's move on. Open your notebooks, please."

৪৩৪৪

"Lizzie didn't understand what I expected from her by this exercise," Rob texted in our chat group. "The boys were in heaven. They made up a story in which the old gypsy had a card with a cryptogram map with instructions on how to find the treasure of her wealthy husband that used to be the king. The town's people decided to kill the king and take his jewelry. But the king was smart. The night before he died, he said: 'They can take away my body but they can never inherit me," and he hid his jewelry box in a place that only his wife knew about. Now everyone has been chasing her to find where the treasure is. LOL. Do you think that I should cut them off the screen for a while? ☺"

"I didn't get a chance to give it to my group yet. I'll do it tonight," said Drew.

"My agents asked me if this was a mysterious map of some construction site that has limitation on a specific commercial area, which is forbidden to the public. They also asked what I am trying to imply here with the story of the gypsy woman.

I reassured them that the whole thing was just an exercise meant to encourage them to think creatively. Eventually they cooperated.

"I enclosed a picture of what they offered. By the way, they are still convinced that this is indeed a construction map of undeveloped cities. There is no other alternative. ☺"

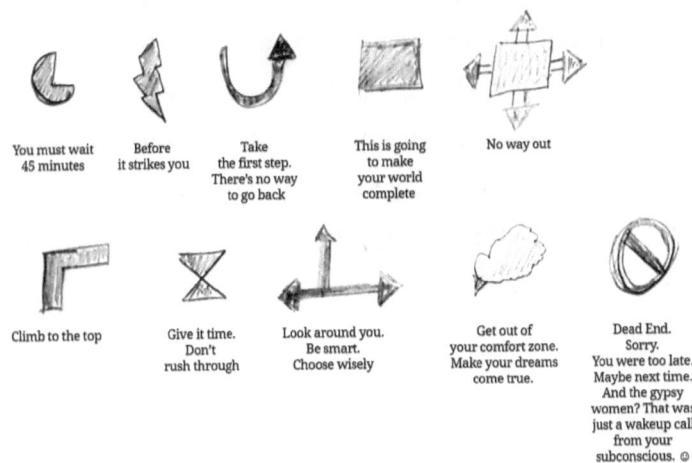

| You must wait 45 minutes | Before it strikes you | Take the first step. There's no way to go back | This is going to make your world complete | No way out |

| Climb to the top | Give it time. Don't rush through | Look around you. Be smart. Choose wisely | Get out of your comfort zone. Make your dreams come true. | Dead End. Sorry. You were too late. Maybe next time. And the gypsy women? That was just a wakeup call from your subconscious. ☺ |

That night I got a bit of an annoyed text message from my sister.

"What's going on with your exercises? My boys keep asking where's the map that dad showed them with the hidden treasure of the gypsy woman? It seems to me a bit too much for eight-year-old boys. Maybe try something on the lighter side next time?"

"You're right," I responded. "I'm sorry. Although, I should think eight-year-old boys these days are much more aware than they were when we grew up. Yet, I have an idea for a nicer one for next week. Something they'd love."

"Okay. I trust my baby brother or should I come again to give you a bath?"

"There is no need, dear sister," I replied. "The memory will remain with me for the rest of my life."

When we were young my sister showed a great interest in animals. One day she read in a magazine that in order to get rid of a bad smell of skunk, you must make a bath with tomato sauce mixed with hydrogen peroxide and baking soda. As a 10-year-old child, I hated nothing more than taking a shower. My sister thought it would be a great idea if she were to bathe me and get rid of my stinky smell. I leave the ending of this story to your imagination.

CHAPTER 8

The phone rang on Eric's desk. He snatched the receiver angrily. "Yes?" His voice was brisk and abrupt.

"Eric?" the woman at the other end inquired.

Eric recognized it immediately. "Oh, I'm sorry, Sydney. Just feeling a bit tense."

Sydney was unruffled; her years of working with the police had taught her that cops get extra tense when working on difficult cases.

"No problem, Eric. I'm calling about Louisa because we had a bit of a drama here."

"Yes. I'm listening. What's going on?"

"I think you should come, Eric. We might have had some kind of breakthrough, but Louisa is in the hospital."

Upon hearing the word "hospital," Eric blurted, "Hospital... what the—"

"Don't worry, don't worry," Sydney interrupted. "She isn't injured, but something happened when she was in the park today, and I think you might be right to be concerned about her safety."

Eric glanced over at Elaine as he continued speaking to Sydney. "We're already on our way." He grabbed the coat Elaine was holding toward him as he hung up the phone.

The detective stopped the car at the hospital's entrance, and Eric noticed that Elaine looked as tense as he felt. They both made their way through the maze of hospital corridors in silence.

In pediatrics, Sydney was waiting for them at the door to Louisa's room. Eric thought she looked a lot more relaxed than he did.

"What happened?" Eric asked looking around Sydney to try and see into the room. The blinds were drawn, but above the bed there was a faint light, and he could just make out the child's tiny silhouette curled up in bed.

"Mrs. Johnson called me this afternoon. Apparently it was a beautiful day, and she took Louisa to the park not far from the house. Louisa was fine, but then Jackie looked over and saw Louisa standing absolutely still and staring across the park toward some bushes. When she tried to see what the child was looking at, Jackie could see a man's head staring back at her. Of course, she started to run across the park immediately, and as she did, Louisa remained silent but pointed toward where the man had been standing. By the time Jackie got there and glanced across, the man was hurrying away. Louisa, though, was completely white and practically paralyzed. When Jackie picked her up, the child suddenly started crying, and Jackie couldn't stop her. It seemed that the girl was in some kind of shock. Not knowing anything about Louisa's medical history, she didn't know what the safest route to take was, so she brought her here and called me."

"She should have called the police," Eric half-muttered to himself, but Sydney overheard.

"She did what she thought was right under the circumstances, Eric. She had to make a couple of quick judgment calls. Remember, we might be dealing with a man who cut a young woman's throat; getting the child out of there seemed top priority."

Eric looked suitably remorseful. "Sorry, Sydney. You're right. It would just have been great to catch him. Did the man do anything? Signal her? Try to approach her? Anything at all?"

"No. Not from what Jackie said, although an officer is interviewing her now. Apparently the man just appeared to be watching Louisa, and we assume that he just looked from a distance while she was playing. Mrs. Johnson couldn't tell how long he was standing there before Louisa noticed him."

"Does Mrs. Johnson think she will be able to identify this man?" Eric asked.

Sydney shook her head. "No. She glimpsed a skinny guy running away when she picked Louisa up but only saw his back. As much as she can remember from what she saw, it looked like a young guy, skinny, dark-skin wearing an old torn shirt."

Eric let out a heavy sigh.

"And the child," he said, straining again to see into the room, "is she okay now?"

Sydney glanced behind her into the darkened room. "They gave her a mild sedative because she appeared to be in some kind of shock. You can talk to her, but since the incident we haven't had a word out of her."

"I'll be gentle with her," Eric smiled.

Sydney looked up and gave his sleeve a small, reassuring tug. "I know you will."

Eric nodded briefly before stepping softly into the room with Sydney and Elaine behind him.

If the truth were known, he felt as if his head was about to explode. Maybe it was because of Missy or maybe because he had another child due any time, but the thought that anyone could possibly target this child filled him with such a rage he had never experienced before. But, for whatever reason, Eric knew he was too close to this case. In fact, he had been from the start. He had to switch back into full cop mode to get to the truth.

Louisa looked like a doll in the large hospital bed. Her black curly hair spread across the white pillow. Eric noticed that not only did the child have an extraordinarily pale complexion but that her attitude had changed and her eyes looked at him wearily as he approached. Mrs. Johnson, he suddenly decided, had done the best thing in bringing her here.

"Hey, Louisa," he whispered. "How do you feel, honey?"

The child's expression didn't change.

Eric tried again. "You remember me?" he said softly. "My name is Eric, and we met when you came to the police station."

The child suddenly looked thoughtful before she said, "Yes." Her voice seemed small and fragile.

"Yes, honey. We had a little chat at the police station before Sydney came to pick you up."

The expression on her face changed, and her eyes filled with tears. "My mommy. Where is my mommy?"

Eric felt his stomach lurch when he realized that, at some point, this child would have to accept that her mommy wasn't ever going to come home.

But Sydney was quick to respond. "Remember, sweetie?" she said, "We talked about it. Your mommy is with the angels in the blue sky now, and she is singing like she always loved to do, just like you told me. She has a white dress and flowers in her hair. And you remember that we said how much she still loves you, that she's always watching over you and always will? Remember?"

"I want my mommy," Louisa screeched amid her sobs.

The adults said nothing. There was nothing to say. Eric resisted the urge to hug her and protect her in the same way he would his own daughter, but he knew that there was one way to keep her safe even if he couldn't return her mother, and that was to catch the man who may be wanting to harm her.

He knelt down at the side of the bed and stroked Louisa's curls gently. "Louisa," he said, in between her gasping intakes of breath, "I really need you to help me."

Eventually, the sobbing started to subside, and the flow of tears stopped before she looked directly at him with a puzzled expression. Eric didn't want to force the child but he knew he had no choice. They had to find out if the man Louisa had seen was a genuine threat or not.

"Louisa, sweetie, the man, the one you saw today," he asked gently. Louisa closed her eyes and blocked her ears with her hands, "A green ghost!" she shouted.

Sydney tried to help. "Eric is a very nice man, Louisa. He's a good friend of mine. He just wants to help us."

But Louisa refused to say anything more and simply shook her head from side to side.

Eric looked helplessly at Sydney. They both knew that the only chance to track down the suspect would be to ask her to identify him, but they both knew that if a three-year-old girl refuses to cooperate, there was not much they could do.

Eric turned around to look at Elaine, but she simply stared back at him and mouthed, "What does she mean 'a green ghost'?" Eric shrugged his shoulders. He was as perplexed as any of them.

"Wait, I have an idea," said Sydney quietly to Eric and Elaine. "Louisa, may I show Eric the beautiful picture you made for me yesterday?"

Louisa nodded while curling further into the bed.

"Here, I'll get it." Sydney went to her purse on the chair next to Louisa's bed and pulled out a white piece of paper and handed it to Eric.

Eric studied it carefully. It was a typical drawing of stick figures as every three-year-old child makes. The picture was drawn with only two colors: black and dark green. He could easily recognize the figure of a girl with curly long black hair that Sydney had titled "Louisa." Next to it was another taller girl figure with long black straight hair with two dark eyes, no nose and no mouth. Sydney had written "Mom" next to that one. But there was a third stick figure, one with big black eyes and short black hair. Next to the third figure was written in Sydney's clear handwriting: "NO NAME."

Sydney looked knowingly into Eric's eyes.

Cautiously Eric held out the picture toward Louisa and pointed at the third figure. "Who is this, honey?" he asked. "Louisa, is this the person you saw today at the park?"

The response was immediate. As soon as she glanced at the drawing, the child did no more than pull the blanket over her head.

Eric felt lost. He knew that there was much more meaning to this stick figure drawing than what was revealed. There was no doubt in his mind that he could find a new lead if only he could crack down the code behind this kid's drawing. As he continued to stare at the drawing, he felt more and more like he was trying to decipher some code, as if he was trying to finish this story in order to solve the murder.

Sydney could read Eric's mind, and she shook her head slowly from side to side. "I'm sorry, Eric. I wish there was something else I could say. I wish there was more," she whispered. "Maybe tomorrow. Come again tomorrow, Eric."

Eric nodded in agreement, but he had at least made up his mind about one thing, and immediately had an officer put on guard at the door of the child's room. Whoever the "no name" or "the green ghost" was, Eric was certain that the person didn't have the child's best interests at heart.

CHAPTER 9

From the darkest mind of a potential killer:

Everyone has a name that was given to them when they were born. The first name was chosen by the parents; the last name is the tribal name. It was picked by the ancestors or the previous generation.

A child will carry that name for the rest of his life, until death.

A name is an identity. It's the symbol of existence in the world.

There's a person in the high above, and his job is recycling the names. If your grandfather's name was Ahmad, then at least one of his grandchildren must be named Ahmad.

A first name has many forms. For your brothers you have one name, but for your relatives, you will always be your proper name. The last name is a whole different story.

The tribal name has a meaning. It's your identity. Someone carved that name onto your crib. Even the person above cannot help you.

Your tribal-family name is not only for your brothers. It's your entire world. This is your universe. It is your responsibility and commitment.

It is set in stone, it is inherited in your blood. No one will dare violate this agreement.

You belong to the tribal family. They determine your future. They are the masters of your fate. They judge. They decide if you live or die. Their sentencing is on your head. If you prove to be loyal, you can earn your life. If you breach the contract, you will be considered dead.

You are your family's property. Your family's name has an owner.

Who are you and who is your master?

CHAPTER 10

"Do you want to hear a joke?" I asked as soon as I walked into the class.

"Yes," the students replied immediately.

"Good. So do I." We laughed.

"So, listen; last night a friend of mine shared a link on social media to a very interesting article about the connection between jokes, health, and the brain. Basically, the article states that most human beings like to laugh out loud. Laughter makes us feel better and healthier. When we laugh our facial muscles relax, our breathing is interrupted, we make unusual sounds and sometimes even breathe hard, right? If we laugh for a long time, we may feel a slight pain in our abdominal muscles, and sometimes tears will show up and our face will turn red. Still, this article insists that's it's healthy to laugh."

"That totally makes sense," someone said. "When I laugh too

much, my stomach hurts."

"True!" I said. "The articles also found that people who use humor frequently are less stressed at work, are more creative, and have fewer conflicts."

"Correct," said another student. "When I get into trouble, I have to be extremely creative to come up with the best jokes to get out of it."

"You're not the only one." I smiled and said, "Did you know that teachers who use humor are more popular among students? Did you know that they are also less burned out from the teaching profession? Yes, the joker of the class is usually considered to be the 'cool' kid, right, Brandon?"

"Heck, yeah," said Brandon. We all laughed. "But not all the teachers get my jokes."

"That's right," I replied. "There may be situations where a person from another culture may not understand our humor. What makes me laugh does not necessarily make you laugh, and believe me, I speak from experience."

"What's the connection to creativity and breakthrough ideas?" someone asked.

I didn't answer directly.

I said, "So, when we understand a joke and laugh at it, we actually perceive a particular situation from different perspectives; we understand the absurdity, and it makes us respond with a 'pause' in our way of thinking. Jokes make us laugh because we are in a situation that breaks our expectations. We are taken by surprise. Jokes usually describe a realistic situation with an unexpected ending to a story. This peculiarity makes your brain 'freeze' or 'pause for a moment' and respond with a smile."

"Is it possible to create this moment intentionally? A moment that will make our brain 'freeze' or 'pause for a second?'" Jen asked.

"The answer is yes," I replied, "and yet, as with other things in life, we need to practice." I paused for a moment. "So, what do you say? Would you like to try it out with our **EXERCISE NO. 4**?"

"Oh yeah," the students replied in unison (anything for a laugh).

"Hey, wait a minute," said Jen. "May I try it? I have an idea for a story that would help us practice an unexpected ending. Can I try?"

"Of course," I smiled. "Go for it."

Jen stood up and walked toward my desk. She pulled out my comfortable chair that has four wheels and then quickly jumped and sat on my desk. We all laughed at the unexpected jump.

"Here's my story," she said in a deep voice.

Three men die and come to the gates of heaven. The angel accepts them and says, "You have three days to be here, but remember, you must never taste from the fruits on the trees."

The garden was full of gorgeous trees, and the smell drove them crazy. So, within a few minutes the first man could not resist and picked a fruit from the tree. A moment later the angel came, and bound the man in chains to an ugly old woman. "This is your punishment," said the angel. "From now on, you will live your life next to her." The other two men kept walking, but the smell really drove them crazy. Within two minutes, the second man could not help himself and gave a small bite into the fruit. Again the angel came and bound the other man to chains next to an ugly old woman. The third and last man swore to himself that he must hold back no matter what the temptation. Suddenly the angel arrived and chained him to a beautiful blonde woman. The man was surprised. "What's going on here?" he asked.

"I don't know about you," the blond said, "but I tasted the fruit..."

Jen finished her story and went back to her seat.

"Excellent story, Jen!" I said and noticed that the students were smiling. "Did you feel the 'pause' when your brain translated the ending of the joke?"

The students nodded.

"Good. So now remember students, always look for the unexpected ending to any story, the punch line, and please stay away from the clichés. The ending doesn't have to be funny. Any unpredictable ending will make our brain 'freeze' for a moment before we respond with 'ah' or a smile. "

CHAPTER 11

Louisa's bed was empty when Elaine and Eric came to visit her the following day. There was no officer guarding the door. Eric was immediately perturbed by this lack of communication. If things were going to change, he needed to know. Why hadn't Sydney told him that she was being released, or better yet, why was his officer being told to change the order given him without Eric's consent. Elaine could immediately see that Eric was not happy and his face was turning the same red color as his mustache.

"Let's ask and see why she isn't here," Elaine said in a calm tone.

"Excuse me, do you know where Louisa James is?" Eric asked a passing nurse.

She pointed to the other end of the hallway. "Try the Kid's Club," she offered.

The Kid's Club was more easily identifiable than usual because the appointed officer was standing outside. Elaine thought he looked bored to tears, and she saw relief and a touch of embarrassment on Eric's face as he realized that everything was going according to his orders.

As the detectives approached, the officer standing outside of the room smiled at the two. "She's inside, sir," he said smiling, before Eric had even gotten close.

When they stepped inside, they were hit by a cacophony of color and noise. A big drawing of a rainbow covered one wall, and another was painted with balloons and teddy bears. Miniature furniture stood around the room amid a scattering of toys, games, and stuffed toys. Louisa, though, was easily located among all of the chaos because she was the only child not moving. She sat at one of the emerald green tables staring at Sydney. Sydney was perched uncomfortably at her side, squeezed a little too snugly into a purple kids' chair. Eric immediately felt sorry for Louisa. Chances are she never played with other children before. She didn't have many social skills. What broke his heart more was that instead of Sydney sitting next to her and helping her acclimate to her surroundings, it should have been Louisa's own mother helping her make friends, and the setting should have been a park and not a hospital play room. Unfortunately for this family, the park had turned out to be a place of suffering.

Eric and Elaine had to weave their way through a variety of scuttling children to get to the table, but at least the atmosphere was conducive to something a three year old would be more likely to appreciate than a darkened hospital room.

"Good morning," Eric smiled at Louisa and Sydney determined not to put a damper on the mood.

"Good morning," replied Sydney in an equally cheerful voice as she patted Louisa on the back.

Louisa looked up from the game and automatically waved hello. Eric was relieved to see that she looked happy and calm, and the trauma of the day before appeared to be forgotten.

"How did you sleep, sweetie?" he asked.

"Okay," said Louisa, shrugging her shoulders.

"Our sleeping beauty here," laughed Sydney, "didn't want to wake up this morning. I had to tickle her." She tickled Louisa again who curled up and giggled.

Eric and Elaine smiled, but in reality their minds were on something quite different. In his pocket, Eric had the coded picture Louisa had drawn the day before. He wanted to use it to try and ask Louisa again about the figures. Yet, how would he do it without getting another negative reaction from the child? Instead, Elaine broke the silence.

"So, what are you playing?" she asked, pointing to the card game on the table.

"Go Fish," Louisa said in an almost inaudible voice.

"Oh, do you like the game?" Eric asked.

Louisa didn't reply. It soon became apparent to the two women that Louisa didn't respond well to men. Especially older men. It dawned on Sydney that perhaps Louisa didn't have her father or any other male figure around, and if she did, he may have been domineering.

"I think she does, but Louisa might be tired now since we have played it for the last hour!" Sydney noted while playing with the ends of Louisa's hair.

"I have an idea! Let's play another game," Elaine said, trying to sound cheerful. She had found a box of cards on the top of a bookshelf and picked them up as she pulled out a small purple chair and sat down at the other side of the little girl.

Louisa eyed her cautiously. "Who you?" she asked.

Elaine held out her hand, but the child didn't move. Elaine took this as a sign that Louisa needed a little coaxing.

"My name is Elaine, and I work with Eric at the police station," she said slowly so the girl could understand her, and then added, "Let's play a game, all of us together. How about that?"

"Game?" Louisa asked hesitantly.

"It's a fun game that I used to play with my nieces," said Elaine. "It's called, 'What Goes With What?'" Elaine then opened the box of cards and laid them out on the table. Each card had a picture on it with the name of the object the card depicted. Elaine continued, "I pick a card, let's say 'flower,' then the person next to me has to find a card that goes with that card." Elaine tried to explain slowly enough that the child would understand. "Okay? Here, I put down flower, and Sydney puts down what?"

"A butterfly! It's just landed on the flower," Sydney explained helpfully as she plucked the butterfly card from the pile.

Louisa's eyes lit up as she looked at all the pictures on the cards. She looked up at Sydney and said, "You."

"My turn?" Sydney said to help Louisa learn the language better. "Okay, I say princess," Sydney said, picking up the card with a drawing of a dark-haired girl wearing a frilly pink dress. "She looks like you." Louisa began watching Eric carefully.

"And I say princess and her prince." Eric pulled out a chair and sat down as he pulled the prince card and placed it next to the princess.

Louisa giggled and clapped her hands. "Me now."

Eric smiled and said, "I pick ... chocolate, and you pick...?"

"This!" Louisa was thrilled as she picked up a card with a picture of a birthday cake on it. She continued, "Me turn."

"*My* turn," Sydney corrected.

"My turn," Louisa repeated. "I pick teddy bear." She was happy when she came up with the card and looked at Elaine. "You say?"

Eric only vaguely heard the girls giggling as they busied themselves playing the game. He took a deep breath. His brain was drilled, and he was getting impatient. Would he ever find a good time to take out the drawing? And, more importantly, how would Louisa respond? Maybe, he considered, it would be better to get help from a child psychologist, someone who specialized in this kind of thing. But, he reasoned, how long would that take, considering there could be a man out there looking to murder this child.

"Eric, it's your turn," Sydney pulled at his sleeve.

"My turn ... for...?" he stammered.

"To pick a card," said Louisa.

"Card ... hmm, right ... a card." Eric had many cards to choose from, but he rejected all of them except one that had a picture of a house on it.

"Home." Eric took a chance and felt the air between them freeze.

All eyes were on the child as the smile drifted from her face along with the color. The silence seemed to last an eternity.

"Home," she repeated slowly.

Sydney spoke up, "It's where you live, honey. Where you lived with Mommy."

Then suddenly an energy seemed to rise within her. "Home!" she cried out. "Home with Louisa, Leila, and Uncle Hamdi!"

Eric felt as if his head was about to explode. Louisa actually managed to complete the story without Eric giving much effort. He felt closer to knowing the end of this entire story, this entire case he felt himself getting too far involved with. Eric felt this new information was something that needed his immediate attention. He could tell Louisa didn't want to talk any more, so he thanked Louisa for playing the game with him, and he and Elaine left.

After the hospital visit, they returned to the station to handle the more mundane cases that had landed on their desks. Eric contacted a source at Immigration and Border Control and gave them the name Hamdi to search in their records for entry into the United States around the same time as Carolyn. Carolyn? Is that who Leila is or is Leila another babysitter or friend who lived with Carolyn? Are Carolyn and Leila sisters, and Hamdi is Leila's husband? A thousand questions were running through his head. Who the hell is Uncle Hamdi?

Eric had to put that case on hold as he quickly brought his attention to the smaller cases in town. There was a complaint about a dispute between two neighbors, and a car accident with a hit and run driver. No injuries, just some bent fenders, but still it took up valuable time.

While driving back home at the end of the day, he focused once again on Louisa. Eric decided to show the child Carolyn's passport photo to see if Leila was indeed Mommy, but he didn't really want to disturb the girl again.

Was the man Louisa saw in the park this Uncle Hamdi? And, if it was, why didn't he approach her and, more to the point, why did she look so scared and then call him a "green ghost"? Why green? What does that color mean? Is it another code? None of it seemed to make sense.

More to the point, Eric thought, *no matter who he is, where the hell is he now?*

"I was thinking the same, Eric," said Sydney when she called him the next day to report that Louisa had been released from the hospital. "I tried every way I could think of to encourage her to speak, but now she's saying she doesn't remember anything and that she doesn't know why she said those names."

"And where is this 'home'?" he asked, "Hope Street or where she came from?"

"She doesn't know, Eric. She has no clue. She's not even four yet, and who knows when and where the girl really came from. Long-term memories in children are not developed at that age."

"I know, damn it, I know." Eric was angry and frustrated. He'd promised to keep Louisa safe. "If someone dares to get close to this girl again, I will..." He didn't finish the sentence. Instead, when he hung up, he assigned a police officer to escort the girl and the foster mom every time they left the house. "And leave the lights on," he told them. "Let them be like those rays of light that reach up to the stars." It was a quote from Missy's favorite book that he used to read to her at bedtime. Now, she was more into princess stories.

On the yellow sticky notes pinned to the board in his office, he added the words:

Mom = Leila. Then he took a thick marker and deleted the words:

Name of the victim = Carolyn James.

It's just a game of words. No more than that.

ℵℜ

"Eric, there's an envelope on your desk," Elaine said as soon as Eric walked into the office the next morning. "The Path Lab sent it over by messenger half an hour ago."

"Thanks," he muttered, before tearing open the package and sliding a small plastic packet containing a gold pendant. A note inside the envelope read: "The only prints and DNA are of the victim." The note was signed by Louis, the technical head at the local autopsy lab.

Eric pulled the string that tied the necklace together and freed the gold pendant. The pendant was small and round like a coin with a golden tree engraving.

He pulled a pen from his shirt pocket and lifted the golden pendant and immediately noted it didn't appear to have much value. He carefully examined the tree image engraved on it. It was a different type of tree with long branches that were rammed one into the other. Not the usual kind of trees you can see in America. A foreign tree.

"What are you doing?" asked Elaine as she approached him.

"I'm trying to figure out what type of tree this is."

Elaine took a closer look at the pendant. "I've never seen anything like it. It's really quite strange."

"Hmm," Eric muttered. "What makes it even stranger is that no one tried to take it out of her pocket until we arrived at the murder scene. We also found that strange ripped piece of paper with weird symbols next to her body on the ground. I wonder if it's significant. The tree and the codes I mean. It looks kind of symbolic."

"You're probably right. I don't think I've ever seen a tree like that before. Maybe we should consult with an arborist?"

Eric looked sharply up at her. "A what?"

"An arborist. A tree expert."

Eric smiled, pleased that he'd called Elaine back to work.

"Hmm...yes, that's a good idea," Eric agreed. "Any thoughts on where we might find one?"

"Botanical gardens might be a good place to start?"

"But," he offered, "an ab...a tree expert won't help if it's just symbolic?"

"Well," she said smiling back at him, "we won't know until we ask, now will we, sir?"

Eric smiled grudgingly.

"I'm trying something new, Elaine," said Eric. "I'm starting to look at the case from the end to the beginning. We have a dead body and we have an unsolved murder case, right? I'm trying different angles now. Here, listen to this. If I find the motive first, I'll have a better chance to track down the trail of the murderer, and if I can do that I can get the real identity of the victim."

"Easier said than done, huh?" Elaine said.

"True," Eric smiled at his partner. "Well, obviously it is not a financial motive. The poor girl had nothing. No use of drugs were found in her body so that rules out that option. Betrayal?

Revenge? Apparently she came from another country and lived under a false identity. Was she kidnapped?"

"Maybe someone kidnapped her and forced her into marriage or maybe he wanted to keep her quiet?"

"Anything is possible."

Elaine peered down into Eric's face. He seemed lost, and she had no clue how she could help.

They returned their attention to the pendant.

"Let's start with an expert of symbols, nature, trees, or God knows what. Who do we have in the system?"

CHAPTER 12

It was Saturday 6:45 a.m. when I read the incoming text message:

Rob is in the hospital. He had surgery last night. He came out from the recovery room, and we're on the way to the orthopedic unit. He wants to see you.

I was nervous.

By 7:08 I was already out of the house. At 7:45 I parked my car in the hospital parking lot and hurried to the 2nd floor. Rob was lying in bed and was somewhat pale. His eyes were closed. The IV was connected to the infusion hanging over his head. His left hand was in a cast raised above his bed inside a metal rack.

"Hey," I kissed my sister on the cheek. "What happened?"

"Our carving artist here decided to carve himself," Miriam grinned with a nervous laugh. "He didn't even feel the cut until the jigsaw was already half way through his arm. Fortunately, he only partially sawed the bone. The surgery took about two hours, and he will recover full use of his arm after some physical therapy."

"Poor Rob," I whispered. "Is he in much pain?"

"He's still under the influence of anesthesia. He was mumbling when he came out of recovery. Something about three men eating forbidden fruits or something like that..."

"I'm not sleeping," said Rob, "and I can hear everything you're saying." He smiled and opened his eyes.

"How are you?" I came closer to his bed. "How do you feel?"

"Glad you came, bro. I must show you something. Do you see this picture?"

I looked around. I had no idea what he was referring to.

"What? Where?" I asked.

"This picture on the TV screen. Look at this commercial. Look now," Rob said.

A small TV screen hung on the top corner of the opposite wall and presented the hospital video network. There were commercials with news headlines that ran across the screen. Rob pointed to one of the advertisements, which dealt with a health drink. On the left side of the picture, slightly elevated in the air, was a simple glass jar filled with a greenish-yellow liquid. On the side next to it, was a large glass with liquid being poured into it.

"You mean the juice of nature?" I read the words that ran on the screen.

"Yes. Exactly."

"Okay." I looked at my sister with a dazed look. *The sedative must have confused this poor guy.*

"This is not just an ad for a drink," he said. "It is running on every TV screen in this hospital. I even saw it in the ER and the prep room for surgery."

"Seems to me that someone is pouring a lot of money here," I said smiling.

"Yes, I think it's funny and a bit ironic to advertise for a health drink just before you go into surgery. A little late isn't it?" He coughed and sighed. "I want you to look back at this commercial. What do you see?"

"We don't have to do it now, Rob," I said, adding, "There's time. Let's get back to it later, when you feel better."

"No," he insisted, "I must show you. It's been driving me crazy since the minute I came in."

"OK, I got it," I gave up.

"Look again at this advertisement."

I waited two minutes and the advertisement appeared on the screen again. I still couldn't figure out what he was referring to.

"I..." I stammered, "I see a jar with juice or iced tea, I guess."

"You're missing it," he insisted, "Look again. It's in the details."

"Okay. I see the juice is poured into a glass, and on the glass are a few drops that are lingering on the outside of the cup.

Perhaps as a symbol of sweat or sports physical effort?"

"Right, go on," Rob urged.

"I see that the green color dominates. Maybe it's healthy green, a hint for nature, eat healthy-natural food, things like that."

"Look at the small signs," Rob tried to hint.

"Signs ... hmm .... I'm looking for...." I had no idea what he wanted me to see. In the meantime, the commercial disappeared.

"Wait for it to come back. There's something that is hidden here like a kind of treasure. If you look really closely, you can see other ideas. Want an example?"

"Yes."

"Look for the arrow going up. In the Runic alphabet, the ancient German language, this arrow was called "Tiooz" and was used as a symbol of a warrior meaning renewal and determination. And look at the little cube, it's named "Aingooaz" and symbolizes ruling, which means rebirth."

I was confused, but not surprised. One of Rob's pastimes was the study of old languages. It seemed to me that the effect of the anesthetic was confusing his thoughts.

"No, I'm not confused and I'm not talking nonsense, and I know exactly the looks on your faces with my eyes closed," he laughed, "but I'm interested to know how come I never noticed these small details before I got here? After all, I have seen this commercial hundreds of times before, but I never really bothered to look closely."

True. I've seen this commercial before, and I'm willing to bet that many other people have as well.

"Advertisements have power over our subconscious," I told Miriam and Rob. "Do you have any idea how many times I bought something that I never intended to buy just because it sounded familiar? But I never bothered to really look at the small details. Who really looks at hints hidden in every advertisement? And, you know what, I'm pretty sure that there are plenty of those."

"So, what do you say?" Rob asked. "Does it fit **Exercise No. 5**?" He smiled. "Let's call it: *what's hidden in the details*—the visible vs the hidden message."

₨ℓ⁓

"Let me clarify a couple of things before turning to Exercise No. 5," I said as soon as I walked into the class the next Monday morning.

"Raise your hand if you have ever seen a movie when all of a sudden the phone rings and the new model phone appears on the screen with its famous logo."

Everyone did.

"How about when a character in the movie is jogging and the camera focuses on his sneakers, and it takes you a second to recognize its brand," said another student.

"Yes. Exactly." Everyone nodded.

"Those are called product placement advertisements," I

explained. "When it comes to commercials, every advertising campaign contains an overt message that is used intentionally and a hidden message that it's upon the observer to figure out.

"So, what you're telling us is that no matter what we look at, there's always a hidden message, and we just need to figure it out?"

"Yes. Exactly," I said. "A hidden message is implied from the text or image, but you should make an effort to find it."

"That will take too much of my brain cells," Brandon said, shaking his head.

We all laughed.

"You know who else is using hidden messages?" I asked.

"Teachers?" someone suggested.

"Yes, absolutely. Just pay attention to what teachers are saying a few days before the final tests. You will find a lot of clues in there," I smiled. "But that's not all. Politicians, for example, use hidden messages quite a lot in their speeches. Hidden messages are not necessarily negative.

You could take advantage of using those hidden messages in your favor. You can implement those codes into someone else's subconscious. Did you know that if you nod your head—yes—during a meeting, the atmosphere will be positive? Interviewers reported that 'this man just gets me.' Just a few small hidden gestures, like those, will send the right message forward."

"Now I'm curious," said someone.

"Just in time," I smiled, "but before I read the instructions, I need two volunteers to act as the interviewer and the interviewee." I pulled Exercise No. 5 out of my bag and read the instructions to the class.

EXERCISE NO.5

Visible and hidden message

Imagine the following situation. You're about to be interviewed for your dream job. You know that you are up against many other talented and qualified candidates. How would you convince the interviewers to choose you and not another person for the job?

Would you be able to plant hidden messages—that you are an original thinker, creative, and have many ideas to solve any issue—in the subconscious of the interviewers?

Pay attention to the rules of the exercise.

Complete the following dialogue in the best way you can; however, do not use the following phrases:

I'm the best, most appropriate, if you choose me (these are three phrases that repeat themselves most often during job interviews and will put you on par with all the other candidates).

Find other ways to plant these hidden messages into the interviewer's mind. Remember, you must be polite, be honest, sincere, and serious. Do not overdo it.

In the following interview we collected the most original

questions that were used in job interviews. Do not answer by yes or no. Do not use routine responses used by hundreds of people before you. Think of another option and be as original as possible.

The situation: There are three people in the professional team of interviewers. They are very nice but very busy. Their company has set them up for 18 job interviews today, and they have three similar days ahead. For every interview, they have allocated 15 minutes. These are also your most critical minutes.

Good luck.

A Job Interview - Different and Very Creative

Interviewers: "Good morning, Mr. .... Please sit down."

Interviewee: "_____."

Interviewers (hold your resume): "Please tell us about yourself in one sentence."

Interviewee: "_____."

Interviewers: "Why should we choose you for this job?"

Interviewee: "_____."

Interviewers: "Why do you want this role?"

Interviewee: "_____."

Interviewers: "Give us an example of your failure, how did you deal with it, and what did you learn from it."

Interviewee: "_____."

Interviewers: "If chosen for this position, what are the first three things you would do in the morning when you get to the office?"

Interviewee: "_____."

Interviewers: "You get to the office and you have more than 100 e-mails waiting for you. You have time to go through just about 30. Who will you answer first?"

Interviewee: "_____."

Interviewers: "If you win the lottery, would you still continue to work?"

Interviewee: "_____."

Interviewers: "What didn't you like about your previous employer? Can you point out three things?"

Interviewee: "_____."

Interviewers: "Let's see how you're doing with original thinking: Why is the Earth round?"

Interviewee: "_____."

"Interviewers:" If there was no force of gravity in the world, what would be different?"

Interviewee: "_____."

Interviewers: "You invented a quick bread-cutting device. The device is great, but there's one problem. Sometimes the knife slips away, and there's a small chance that it may injure people. Fixing the device costs half a million dollars, and you have no way to raise that amount of money. What would you do?"

Interviewee: "_____."

Interviewers: "If I were to ask you how many Labrador dogs are in Brazil, how would you answer?"

Interviewee: "_____."

Interviewers: "Excellent. And one more question: What's your favorite scent and why?"

Interviewee: "_____."

The interviewers stand up and shake your hand: "Thank you for contacting us Mr. X. We'll be in touch soon."

Interviewee: "Thank you very much for taking the time to meet me today. I am looking forward to hearing from you. Good Day."

ഓരു

Drew hadn't gone out on a date recently, at least not for several months. Not that Drew had any problem finding pretty girls. He, himself, was a very attractive guy. He had the look of a lawyer, tall, broad shoulders, and fair with somewhat long hair. He had the manners of a gentleman, and cheek dimples that melted women's hearts whenever he smiled. It was not surprising, then, that smart and attractive women were captured by his charm.

After his last marriage ended in divorce, Drew simply refrained from getting into another serious relationship. Occasionally, young women approached him and invited him for a date. He welcomed the approach and responded positively. He was happy to meet them for a drink at the bar but refused politely and stubbornly for a second date.

While drinking his coffee this morning, he opened up the blinds and let the bright sun in. When he reached out to grab his jacket to head to work, a note fell from the pocket. He bent down and picked it up. It took him a second to remember that the note was a phone number of the smiling girl he met last Tuesday at the fitness center. He was a member there but visited rarely.

Why not, he thought as he dialed her number.

"Good morning," she answered after two rings.

"Cheryl? Good morning. I hope you remember me. This is Drew, the handsome guy from the fitness club." He laughed.

"Of course, Drew. Good morning. How are you?"

"Excellent. I hope this is a good time. I woke up this morning and saw this wonderful spring weather and it winked at me."

"Are you on the way to the gym?" she asked.

"No, no, I'm sorry, I'm actually just getting ready to go to work. I have a meeting in an hour but thought to be spontaneous and invite you for lunch today. I mean, if you're not busy?"

"Lunch?" She was surprised. "I thought you didn't commit to more than a drink?"

Drew laughed, "I see that you checked up on me, huh?" He laughed again.

"Yep, something like that," she confirmed.

"Actually, it's kind of true. Usually I don't meet for more than a drink, but today I felt like doing something else. To celebrate this gorgeous sunshine! So, what do you say? Let's buy chili dogs and go for a walk in the park. I mean, with this kind of weather, it's such a shame to get stuck between four walls."

"You just know how to convince a lady, huh?" Cheryl laughed. "Okay. I'm with you. Love the idea of being outdoors."

Drew hung up the phone and smiled. What does it matter if it's a drink date or a meeting between friends in the park? To break the routine once in a while was a good thing. He turned his key ring around his finger and locked the door behind him.

The weather was wonderful. Pleasant rays of sun caressed them as they walked along the paths in the park. Luckily, neither of them suffered from allergies, so they could enjoy the colorful blossoms and the aroma at the beginning of spring.

Drew chatted a little bit about his work, enjoying Cheryl's company. They gobbled chili dogs and shared a bag of potato chips.

Drew was curious when Cheryl talked about her hobby of climbing mountains. She admitted that her dream was to climb Kilimanjaro. "It was also my father's dream," she said.

"So why haven't you done it yet?" he asked.

"I don't know, neither one of us got a chance. I guess we both haven't found the right time yet."

"I believe in dreams," Drew admitted, "even though I'm a lawyer." They laughed.

"Lovely day," said Cheryl, lifting her gaze to the wispy clouds overhead. "Drew, you were right. It's such a shame to waste it indoors."

They walked in silence for a moment.

"So, Drew, tell me more about yourself."

"Sure, what do you want to know?"

"Hmm.... I don't know, like, where did you grow up? Why did you choose law school? And how come no woman has captured your heart by now?"

Drew laughed.

"Let's start with the simple things. I was born and raised in the suburbs of D.C., a nice neighborhood in Maryland. I'm the youngest of three mischievous boys. I got the beauty, the others got wisdom."

She smiled. "What do your brothers do?"

"Bobby is a chief scientist at NASA; he was always a bit of an astronaut. He lives in California with his wife Katie and their five cats."

"Wow!" she exclaimed. "Quite a lot of cats."

"Yes, I know. We're always making fun of them that someday when they have a child, they'll get him a sandbox instead of a toddler bed."

They laughed, and Drew noticed she was especially attractive when she laughed.

"Is Bobby the oldest?"

"Yes, Bobby is the oldest, followed by Richard, older than me by a year and a half."

"My brother is also named Richard. We call him Richie," said Cheryl. "He's older than me by almost two years."

"I always suspected that we have something in common,"

Drew said with a wink. "Either that or all older brothers are named Richard." He paused to finish the last bite of his hot dog. "What does your Richie do?"

"He's a detective, Area 34. He lives in New York with his wife and daughter," she replied.

"Really? Homicide?"

"Yes," she said. "He loves his job. What about your Richie?"

"The truth is that my Richie does something somewhat similar. He's a forensic pathologist with NYPD, looking for the cause of death."

Drew felt that the atmosphere became a bit heavy and decided to change topics. "May I ask you something?"

"Of course," she replied.

"If you could do something else, anything in the world, what would you do?"

"Hmm...an interesting question. You mean in terms of a career? Actually, I feel good about my position. I started working for the fitness center about eight years ago and was certified as a yoga instructor. I feel comfortable, I know everyone, know what to do, and how to face problems."

"And wouldn't you like to move on? I don't know, maybe like run your own yoga studio?"

"Not really. At the moment it suits me. There are sometimes problems and urgent things to be solved, but overall it's peace of mind, you know. I come to work, do the best job I can, and go back to my apartment."

"Interesting," said Drew.

"Why?"

"I feel the same way. In general, I'm happy where I am now. I'm not a partner in the firm, I'm not an associate, I'm just a "hired" lawyer, but I'm actually happy this way. My benefits are good, and it's an established firm. I have no ambition to be independent and to run an office of my own. Sometimes I wonder what would have happened if I had worked in different jobs every week, you know, like one week cleaning horse stables, the next week fishing in a rowboat..."

"This is definitely interesting, as you said." Cheryl tittered. "Just don't count on me to clean out the stables."

They laughed.

"Tell me something, Cheryl, what's your favorite smell?"

"Smell?" She looked as confused as she felt.

"Yes. What's your favorite smell?"

"Hmmm...smells that I like...maybe the smell of the wet grass after the rain, you know, when everything is clean and smells of fresh air."

"And what if I were to ask you, how many Labrador dogs are in Brazil. How would you answer?"

"Dogs? In Brazil? Drew, what's wrong with you?"

"Nothing, it's just a game. What would you say?"

"Hmm...I would say I have no idea and I have to search Google for the answer. I'm sure some crazy guy already tested it out. But...why do you ask?"

"And just one more question: why do you think that the earth is round?"

"Drew, that's really weird." She looked at him curiously. "I mean, why are you asking me these questions? I don't really understand..."

"Nothing, really. I just ran into a sort of questionnaire preparing people for a job interview, and there were all those questions. You know, not the usual type of questions asked during a job interview. It made me curious to find out how people would respond to them."

Cheryl glanced at the clock and was startled.

"Oh, Drew, I'm really sorry, I really have to run. One of the aerobics instructors called in this morning asking me to cover her classes. I wanted to do some stretching before class. Is that okay? I mean, if you'd like, I'll be happy to meet again and answer all your questions, but I have to run now."

Drew wasn't sure what to say. On the one hand, Cheryl was a nice person, and on the other hand, he avoided going out on a second date. He knew a second date had more of a romantic hint.

"Okay. I'll call you tonight and we'll set something up," he called out while she rushed back to the gym. She waved goodbye.

He chose to walk slowly from a bypass trail back to the office. The sun smiled.

CHAPTER 13

Eric's phone extension beeped incessantly.

"Yes?" said Eric.

"Mr. Jum'a is here," George informed him.

"Mr. Who?"

"Jum'a. He's on his way up."

Eric tapped on the glass window that separated his and Elaine's office and asked her to come in.

Mr. Jum'a leaned on his cane, barely able to drag his feet. He was a chubby man, probably in his 80s, Eric estimated, wearing a brown faded suit with matching hat and carrying a small leather case. His round face was sweaty and reddened with the effort of negotiating the stairs, and his thick glass spectacles were slipping down to perch precariously on his nose, which was now slick with perspiration.

Eric rushed to support his arm, and pulling out a chair,

helped the old man carefully into it.

"Thank you. Thank you," Mr. Jum'a whispered before pulling off his hat and mopping his forehead and bald pate with a cloth handkerchief.

Eric glanced at Elaine as she left the room only to return seconds later with a glass of water.

"Thank you," the old man said again, and then everyone fell into silence until he'd finished the glass.

"How can I help you, sir?" Eric asked when the old man's color had settled down to something close to normal.

"I came to help you," said Mr. Jum'a. "Where is it? Where is the pendant?"

"Where is...? What?" Eric was confused.

"Oh, I'm sorry," Elaine jumped in. "Eric, I'm sorry, this is Mr. Jum'a. The arborist I contacted yesterday to help us identify the tree on Carolyn's pendant. I forgot to tell you he was coming in today."

"Oh, I do apologize," Eric said shaking Mr. Jum'a's hand. "Thank you so much for coming. I guess I was expecting... expecting..." Eric's voice trailed off.

"Someone younger?" Mr. Jum'a offered.

Eric simply smiled in response.

"I'm retired, or try to be," Mr. Jum'a explained, "but your problem did appear to be rather interesting for me, so the manager at the botanical gardens gave your officer here my name. My years of studying trees have also led to me being a semiotician."

"Excuse me?" Eric asked.

"A semiotician is someone who is an expert in symbols and communication. I have been called upon to look at many trees in the realm of symbolism. A perfect fit you might say for what you are looking for."

"Well," Eric replied, "I'm, we're, certainly pleased to have the assistance of an expert." Then before anything else could be added, he took the white envelope from his desk drawer and slipped the pendant gently into Mr. Jum'a's outstretched hand.

The old man stared at the small object for a few seconds before suddenly becoming very business-like. He pulled out a small red velvet jewelry display pad from the leather bag and with delicate dexterity skimmed over the pendant and fixed it straight on the padded board. Then he peered into the bag again and pulled out a device that had two circular magnifying glasses in a black metal box. Next came a *loupe*—a magnifying lens, which he planted firmly on top of the glasses.

Eric and Elaine exchanged glances but said nothing.

Mr. Jum'a was ready. He brought the velvet pad closer and stared at the pendant.

"Ummmm," he muttered before turning the pendant over. Another long moment passed before he muttered again, "Ummmm..."

Elaine and Eric waited patiently, occasionally glancing at each other but afraid to make any noise that would disturb Mr. Jum'a's concentration. A few more minutes passed until he turned the pendant over once more.

Finally, the old man stood up and pointed to the reading lamp on Eric's desk.

"May I?" he asked.

"Of course."

Mr. Jum'a gently placed the padded board with the pendant on the table under the lamp and examined the pendant once more. Then, he pulled a long and extraordinarily fine metal pointer from his jacket pocket.

"Is there anything?" Eric asked gently, his patience about to run out.

"It's interesting," the old man said.

"What's interesting?" Elaine asked.

"This is a desert tree, one that grows in hot and dry climates. It can survive the scorching weather. In any case, this umbrella-shaped tree with a high trunk and treetop is covered with leaf-like thorns. I can't tell you specifically what it is. Many trees and plants are only clearly identifiable by the leaves, and this engraving is very detailed but too small for fine specifics; however, it's certainly one of the acacias."

"In which country can you find this tree?" Eric asked.

"I'm sure in south-central Africa, possibly in Australia, and in several hot countries. Pretty sure that Iran and Iraq have them too."

"It doesn't really help us," Eric sighed and looked at Elaine. "She could have lived on any of these continents or accepted it as a gift from someone who lives there."

"Hold on," Elaine said, "is there anything else you see on here, Mr. Jum'a? We really need clues."

Mr. Jum'a had returned to staring intently at the pendant. "Well," he muttered, "there might be something else here, although you are not looking at it from a botanical perspective, but rather a cultural one."

Eric leaned forward, straining to look over the old man's shoulder. "Cultural? What can you see Mr. Jum'a?"

Without turning around Mr. Jum'a beckoned them both forward with a wave of his hand. "See here," he said, moving the fine pointer to an area on the top half of the pendant. They both leaned forward, but it was impossible to see anything at such a distance.

"You see?" the old man said again and traced the area with his pointer. Eric and Elaine followed the outlines as Mr. Jum'a moved the pointer over the pendant, but neither could make out anything in particular. What exactly were they supposed to be looking at?

Mr. Jum'a marked again with a long pointer the route between the branches of the tree. Eric and Elaine watched in silence. They had no idea what they were supposed to be looking at. Finally, Elaine dared to ask, "What are we supposed to see?"

"It's not what you see immediately that matters."

Eric and Elaine exchanged a glance.

Elaine shook her head. "I'm sorry Mr. Jum'a, but I really don't understand what you mean?"

"Try again," said Mr. Jum'a, adding, "Don't give up. Not always are the answers so prominent."

"Wait a minute," Elaine said suddenly excited, "I think I see something! Look!"

Eric leaned a little further forward and screwed up his eyes, "Where? What?"

"Here, look here," she pointed. "It's here, outside the tree, the area between the edges of the branches and the velvet frame. Do you see it, Eric?"

Eric stared intently at the area Elaine was pointing out. Slowly he began to see all kinds of strange shapes. "I see something here," he muttered. "Two lines that connect at the edge. Right?"

"Yes. True," said Mr. Jum'a. "It's an ancient sword used by knights, called Sa'eif in Arabic. They were common in the 16th century. Today we see them mainly used for ceremonial purposes only."

"So, what would be the significance of a sword like that today?" Eric asked.

"Well, all kinds of people used this Sa'eif in the past. Most people actually, particularly those who lived in the desert and used it as a weapon for hunting. It was an essential tool for nomadic tribes. But it also has a cultural significance."

"What cultural significance?" Eric asked with an air of contempt. He began to think Mr. Jum'a was not as much of an expert as he claimed to be.

Mr. Jum'a simply looked up at Eric with a resigned expression. "First of all, sir, as I have said, my work has allowed me to become a kind of expert in symbols. I used to work at the ancient artifacts department at the archeological museum before I became the public program manager of the botanical gardens.

"Also, I think you would appreciate, officer, that in many eastern countries, knowledge of artifacts used by our ancestors often gets passed down to contemporary generations. Besides, this particular sword is renowned and still used for ceremonial purposes today. It is a little like you recognizing a blunderbuss."

Eric said nothing but simply looked suitably chastised. The old man had made him feel like a small child. Eric also had no idea what a blunderbuss was.

"But," Mr. Jum'a went on, "there's also something else. You see this symbol?" He pointed to an area not far from the sword.

"Barely," Eric replied with caution.

"Try again," said Mr. Jum'a and passed Eric the lens he was holding on his glasses. "What do you see now?"

The amplification was amazing. Suddenly Eric's whole world involved only the small pendant and its intricate drawing. Now he could clearly see the sword and to the right of it was an animal etched into the metal. "It's definitely an animal," he said. "Looks like a horse to me. One of the more delicate-looking horses, like they use for trap racing."

"True," Mr. Jum'a agreed. "It's a horse. More like a noble horse, which is considered part of the family in nomadic tribe cultures."

"Wait," Eric said, "I can see something else as well. It looks like circles just to the left of the horse."

Mr. Jum'a sat back, looking suitably pleased with himself.

"Yes, it's circles of a sort. It's called *Alarg'h* in Arabic, and, before you ask, Detective Gutenheim, it's a kind of headband that women wear that is decorated with coins or metal rings, usually on their wedding day."

"Their wedding day?" Eric said somewhat befuddled. "Wait, does that mean... Leila was married!?"

Mr. Jum'a gave a slow nod. "That is certainly what the inscription would suggest, yes. These are all tiny wedding symbols. The groom gets the Sa'eif on his wedding day in order to protect his family. The horse is a sign of money and pride and, of course, we have the *Alarg'h*. It looks like the pendant was given to the bride on her wedding day to remind her of the specific roots of the culture she came from."

Eric sat down heavily in a chair before asking, "So, do you know where these roots might be, Mr. Jum'a?"

"It all feels like some kind of secret code," Elaine added.

"Wait!" Eric jumped from his seat. "Speaking of codes..." He rushed to his drawer and pulled out the ripped page with the weird symbols that he found next to the body. He handed it over to Mr. Jum'a, "Is it relevant? Can you find a hidden message in it? What does it say?" Eric hoped for some answers.

"Well," Mr. Jum'a smiled. "What I can read in here is not

necessarily the same as what you may see in it," he explained.

"Huh?" Eric asked, a puzzled look on his face.

"Well... Let's look at it from another angle, shall we? I am looking at this particular problem from a cultural, rather than professional, perspective." Mr. Jum'a was choosing his words carefully. "So do not hold me to providing you with the exact answer and interpretation, and," he continued, "I'm not 100 percent certain, but I think we are referring to the roots of the Bedouin culture. But there's something else." He hesitated.

"What is it?" asked Elaine gently.

"There's a famous legend about the Bedouin tribes. The Bedouin are actually one large ethnic group that is formed by many smaller tribes. Everyone thinks it's like a one big happy family, but not many know the real story. Many years ago, during the 18th century or so, one tribe had to be split into two separate groups due to a huge quarrel. This new tribe had to reinvent its own identity. They wanted to stay part of the Bedouin as an ethnic group, but, at the same time, they wanted to adopt their own symbols. They created a new symbol with three heads: one head for the sword that symbolizes the power, another head is the noble horse that symbolizes the belief and values, and the third head is for the coins that symbolize wealth. However, as you can see, all those heads are connected to the tree, because the tree symbolizes the roots of the Bedouin, while the tribes are its branches. This tribe is called the Al-Miiarkh tribe. The daughters of the Al-Miiarkh tribe receive this pendant on their wedding day and must wear it at all times. It's a symbol of their identification. It is unlikely that this object would find its way to the hands of an English woman unless she is a daughter of the Al-Miiarkh tribe. Also, these symbols on this paper are almost reminiscent of hieroglyphics. I think maybe this is all starting to tie together."

ℬↃℭↄ

The detective thanked his good fortune. Google knew who the Al-Miiarkh tribe was. The roots of the early Al-Miiarkh tribe were found in the early 18th century following a tribal feud. The Iben-Daud family was blamed for stealing herds of goats belonging to their neighbors from the same tribe. A huge blood feud was about to begin when the Sheikh (the tribe's leader) was called in. He ordered that the Iben-Daud family be exiled together with their descendants from the same father. They were forced to leave the main Bedouin tribe and flee to the Kalahari Desert in south- central Africa.

The Iben-Daud family did as it was ordered. They packed up their few provisions, tents, camels, as well as their wives and children, and searched for a new settlement place. After many disappointments, the tribe eventually settled with their tents in the south of the Kalahari Desert, a place where many other tribes had also made their home. They were known as "bushmen" or "San people" or "people without property." The tribes hunted, fed mainly on meat, drinking camel's milk and eating their flesh, making water-bags (*Nods*), tents, prayer rugs (*Sajada'*), and shoes from camel skin or camel hair (*Weber*).

Some archeologists argue that the Al-Miiarkh tribe assimilated into another non-nomadic tribe, but their people kept some of the nomadic symbols that were unique. Archeological remains found in the Kalahari Desert included: carved stone sculptures, swords (*Sa'eif*) that were used for hunting, and clay pots used to store the water drawn from the wells.

The Al-Miiarkh tribe mainly observed the Koran restrictions but also worshiped idols, especially the idol of rain and desert winds. They married among themselves and later assimilated into another tribe. They believed in a modest life. Marriages were determined by the tribes' elders and were set with the birth of the baby, reflecting the family's honorable roots.

They valued hospitality and keeping the family's honor, to the death.

In 1961, a central Kalahari Reserve was established in order to preserve the tradition of the tribes who still live in the desert.

By 5:00 a.m., Eric had read everything he could find on the Al-Miiarkh tribe.

The pendant

CHAPTER 14

From the darkest mind of a potential killer:

Love. A simple word of four letters. It's tattooed to your heart. It is burned with metal letters into your skin with heat. One by one you placed them onto your soul. Now it is with you – Forever.

Love hits suddenly. Unplanned. Eyes meet. Looks exchanged. Silence.

It's like a sword that hurts you. The poison drips into your body. It's a dead end. No way out. You are captivated. It's your prison.

That which gives you the most pleasure, gives you the most pain.

Rolling the desired name on your tongue.

Then again whispers the name gracefully. It's soft, tender, has a sweet sound. Pronouncing the name into you. Swallowing it with every breath. Then it becomes part of you.

In your dreams you cry out for that desired name. Demands for its return. Screaming it in your sleep, and with your last breath whisper it softly.

When a person cannot fulfill his love, he gets crazy like a wild animal, waiting for an opportunity to attack. Then you see your chosen one passing by. Bare feet tap gently on the gravel. Trembling hands. Holding pots. Jellabiya and long dresses. Keffiyeh covering heads, protecting from the sun. Shawls covering faces. Only the dark eyes are exposed.

You unexpectedly meet again. Panics. The eyes peek, terrified, and yet so pretty. You dare to stare for a second and then lower your eyes like a modest one should do. You must obey the rules. Oblige your ancestors.

The next time is less restrained, less surprised. Accept fate. The look in the eyes is gentle but persistent.

You separate without words.

You refuse to give up. You wait for your desire

d one for almost a year. Days in, days out. Dreams of conquer haunt you. Finally a surrender. Letting a smile slip out. You are captured. You fall for the charms. It feels like walking on air.

You must do the right thing. You must follow the proper rules.

You long to feel the loving touch.

Now you know. You want to live the rest of your life next to your chosen one.

Satan's bitter laughter. Cruel incarnation of Fate. The father laughs, mocking your foolishness.

Jamal is scornful and mocking. "It's not meant for you. Never will be. I am the eldest brother. I have the right. The sovereignty is mine."

Stinging pain in silence. The cruel dream that was parted. Could it be?

Never?

Who will defeat the agony?

Only death can redeem the pain.

Then death shall be the answer.

CHAPTER 15

One morning, after class, Johnny approached me. Johnny is in his junior year and has been taking my classes for the past three semesters. Johnny finds great interest in literature and decided to continue with me in my advanced writing classes.

"Can I talk to you for a few minutes alone?" he asked.

"Of course," I replied. "Walk with me to the library? We can find a quiet corner there."

I saw a look of desperation in his eyes, which is very unusual for Johnny. Johnny is not just one of my best students he is quite a unique person, too. If a student is having difficulty in class, Johnny will be the one who volunteers to stay after class and help him out. He is the one who greets everyone in the hallways, including the maintenance staff, and will not hesitate to reach out to give a helping hand. He is always there to comfort, encourage, and support in times of need.

"What's going on?" I asked when we walked out into the hallway.

"I want to be part of this," he stated.

"Part of what?" I didn't understand.

He took a deep breath. "I saw the email you sent to the parents at the beginning of the year," he said, "and I saw the exercises you bring to class. I must have more of these."

"More of what exactly?" I still didn't understand.

"These exercises that show you're smart, you know."

"Why? I mean, I'm already bringing them to class anyway, you saw for yourself. When I have an exercise I usually open Monday morning's class with it. You were in all the classes until now, right?"

"Yes, I was, but you don't understand." He paused.

I realized he was searching for the right words.

"What is going on, Johnny?" I placed my hand on his shoulder. "Come on," I found a comfortable seating area. "Let's sit down. Tell me what's going on."

We sat down. Johnny dropped his bag on the floor. He was breathing heavily, and I could see something was definitely bothering him. He looked down at the floor.

"They fired my dad from work about a week ago. I don't know exactly what happened. His boss called him into the office and said something about money that had disappeared. Not just petty cash; it was a fortune. They also filed a lawsuit against him. Now there is an investigation. I know my dad, and I know he didn't do anything wrong, but now he has to give everything he owns to prove that he's innocent. Mom hopes the truth will win in the end, but that's a lot of money he needs in the meantime to pay for the lawyer. We will have to cut down on things, take a second mortgage on the house. Maybe we'll have to move to a smaller place. It doesn't matter. We'll manage."

"I'm so sorry to hear that. Is there anything I can do to help?"

"Actually, there is. It's about those smart exercises."

"Johnny, I'm sorry, I'm not sure what you're thinking, but these exercises are not meant to prove how smart you are. These exercises, my friends and I come up with, are based on principles that stimulate your brain to generate ideas, to help you think differently. That's all. Nothing more."

"OK, so I must have them," he repeated.

"Why?" I was confused.

"Okay. Listen," he sighed. "So I told you that my father lost his job and we have no money."

I began to understand. Johnny will soon be 17. By next year he, like all of his friends in school, will submit their applications for college. His only chance to continue his studies is by being offered a full scholarship.

"Do you understand? If I write my scholarship essay in a different way, suggest an innovative-genius idea that I came up with, that stands out from the hundreds of students applying for the same scholarships, maybe there's a chance that they will want me. Without a scholarship I'll never be able to go. I know that I'll have to work hard, take classes, and work after school to help Mom and Dad financially. I know I can get good recommendation letters attesting my kindness to others, but kindness doesn't help you pay for school, does it?"

I was quiet for a while. I wasn't sure what to say.

Finally I said, "Listen, Johnny, you're a great boy, but you must understand that *The Pencil Pro*, as I wrote earlier this year, is an experimental project. We jot down the exercises during the semester as we go and as I stated before, this is only an addition to our curriculum. In the final exams and the other tests is where you demonstrate your ability. If you keep good grades, and a high SAT score, I'm sure..."

He interrupted me, "But here," he pulled out a print out of the email I sent all the parents on October 16th and read out loud:

I am committed to encourage the students to think and create in various educational means that are available to us. During the coming semester we will add onto our curriculum original thinking exercises to help students develop and stimulate their thinking process while seeing the world in a large variety of colors...

"Are these your own words?"

"Yes, they are," I admitted.

"So, that's exactly what I need!"

"Listen, Johnny, you must understand that this is not a magic formula. This is not a 'magic pill.' Yes, I know it works, it stimulates the brain to generate more ideas through educating it, but you need patience and practice, and you need to keep an open mind. All right?"

Johnny was still looking a bit disappointed.

"But I can do something else for you," I said, "My friends and I usually share these exercises and ideas in our group chat. I'm ready to have you join our group. You'll be like one of the guys. You'll get the exercises first. OK?" I added with a smile.

"Thank you," Johnny said, all smiles. His eyes expressed sincerity and gratitude. "I promise not to disappoint you. I will bring the best innovative ideas."

"This is not a competition," I warned him, using my teacher's tone. "All ideas are equally good."

"Cool!" He picked up the bag from the floor and said, "May I be excused?"

"Dismissed," I replied. I smiled back and saluted him just like in the army.

Not only was Johnny added to the group, but Rob also asked our permission to bring in his two older brothers, and Drew brought a few friends. Slowly, our team grew to 15 members.

"The only thing I request," I wrote in the group chat, "is that whoever joins us brings his own originality, thoughts, and ideas. Do not repeat what someone already said because it makes sense. Bring what sounds like a great idea to you; look at things as if you never saw them before. Let yourself think like a kid again, where everything is possible and there are no restrictions, no force of gravity, and budget doesn't matter. Let your brain take the lead."

Two weeks later our group chat reached its maximum capacity.

"Maybe we should open a Facebook page?" Rob suggested.

"Not a bad idea," I texted him back. "I'm happy to set up a Facebook page for those who are interested."

Our Facebook page was born that day close to midnight. I borrowed a pencil image from Google and sent invitations to all my friends to like us.

On the page *Setup* I wrote:

"**The Pencil Pro** is a pilot project. It is intended to promote original and creative thinking for ages 16 and up. On this site we will present exercises and guidelines to encourage you to think differently. All we ask in return is that you comment and share your own ideas with us. We will be happy if you invite your friends to join this group."

By morning there were 157 members in our group. After another 24 hours, we crossed the threshold of the 1000 followers. We knew we had a hit.

80C3

Yesterday, Johnny approached me after class, "I have an idea," he said.

"I'm listening," I replied.

"How about instead of making us wait until next Monday, when you come in to class with a new exercise, you record yourself on a video and upload the file to YouTube?"

I like watching YouTube clips. I enjoy funny short clips, country music clips, and the replay of old TV shows that are no longer on the air.

"Hmmmm...interesting idea," I said. "I never tried it. How hard is it, technically I mean?" I hesitated.

"That's easy," he laughed. "I can send you a link with instructions. It will take you literally two seconds to upload the file."

"I need to think about it," I said. "I've never done it before."

"Exactly," he winked. "Try new things. Find alternatives. Break the patterns of ideas." He laughed and then said, "What do you have to lose?"

Later that night I sat in front of my laptop. I was ready. I double clicked on the camera button. "The next exercise," I said in a loud and clear voice, "is called: *only 24 hours and everything looks different.*"

EXERCISE NO. 6

Only 24 hours and everything looks different

At times, we all want to be someone else, just for a short while, not forever. Who wouldn't like to switch places with that man across the street and see how this world looks elsewhere? To be the big boss for a day, the mayor, an employee in a burger chain, a teenage boy or girl, a toddler, or even homeless with no mortgage, but just for one time and then go back to our own familiar world.

The following exercise allows us to experience that opportunity. Note that in the next 24 hours you are the same but different. Let's try it out. But, where do we start?

You wake up in the morning, what's the first thing you do? Wait! Not so fast. Are you heading to the bathroom to brush your teeth? Pay attention, which hand are you using to hold the brush? Right hand? Just for the next 24 hours replace it. Try holding it with your left.

Getting dressed? Good! Start with the socks. What color are they? Now match the outfit to the socks. Why? Why not? Come on, give it a chance, maybe you'll find something else you like to do in not the same way.

Breakfast? No, not the same old thing again. I'm sure the refrigerator will be happy to let you try something new. Choose something else from the menu, but remember this is the most important meal of the day.

How do you take your coffee? How about changing the hand holding the mug, and perhaps even the tilt angle? Try! Maybe you'll like it.

Hitting the road? Let's go! Are you on your way to work? Excellent. No, wait a minute, don't go this way, you have already taken this road too often. Today, you replace your neighbor across the street and take the other road. Heck, maybe you'll discover a new path.

Remember that girl in the office? Yes, the quiet one. You have no idea when she comes to work every morning, and what's her last name? Excellent. Usually, you won't inquire about her, but today your alter ego will do just that. Go ahead. Ask her. You have less than 24 hours. Do it.

What's the first thing you do when you get to work? Wow! It sounds really interesting, but just for once try that. Today start with the third thing you usually do and then go back to the second and first. Why? Why not? What do you have to lose?

Did you bring in your lunch today? Excellent. I hope that it would be delicious. Now, go to your colleague and switch trays with him. Yes, you heard me right. Just for today offer him to change places with you at lunch (and maybe even the brave among us will dare to switch their laptops or cell phones?) only 'til the end of the day. Be someone else. Switch your identities. It's only a loan. We promise to return it in a few hours.

Eat something that you didn't plan for today. Try a different flavor. You never know when you may discover something you really like.

Wait, we're not done yet. Here are a few tricks to think about while you still have time.

The English alphabet has 26 letters. The Hebrew language has 22 letters. Russian has 33 letters. There are 29 letters in Spanish, whereas Italian has 21. Did you know that some letters stayed on the editor's floor? Now it's your turn. Try to come up with the next letter that didn't make it to the final stage. The one you think is missing. What is it? What does that letter look like? Let's take it one step forward, how about making some new words?

Are you on your way home? Excellent. Pay attention to road signs. Yes, yes those warning signs that are known to all of us from the driving test. What sign do you think is missing? No, it doesn't have to be related to the road on which you're driving right now, it can be at any milestone. Want an example? Here you go. Please add a signpost before the crosswalk: "Driver Beware! The people crossing the road do not pay attention. They are busy writing text messages."

So, how was your day? Are you back home? Welcome! No, we're not done yet. It's time for dinner. Didn't have time for grocery shopping, huh? Never mind, we can help you. Go into the kitchen. Make yourself the most amazing, inventive, winning pizza. Don't worry, use a piece of bread instead of dough. Don't forget the rolling pin. Now you have the dough for pizza. What to put on the pizza? Yes, everything goes. We won't tell anyone. Be creative. Show us your mix and match. By the way, have you found a name for your winning recipe? That's okay, you have about seven minutes to think about it till your pizza is ready.

That's it. Our 24 hours experiment is almost over. Just one more exercise and we must go to bed.

It's nighttime. Are you tired? Before we wish you good

night, we would like to remind you to get into the opposite side of the bed. Do you usually take the right side? Excellent, just this time try the left, or even better yet, try to put down your head to face the other side of the room, so your head is where your feet used to be. Yes, maybe it will take you another minute to fall asleep this way, but don't forget, tomorrow you will be a different person entirely.

The eyes are closing slowly? Excellent, this is exactly the time to launch the next exercise. No, there is no need to get up or to get pen and paper. This exercise is all about your imagination and preferably with your eyes closed.

Imagine a straight white line on a black background. However, this line is playful. It can't stay straight for a long time. The line rises rapidly climbing up and falling down. A moment later it's spinning in circles in the air. But wait, what is it doing there? No, I don't know. It's all in your imagination. Keep it up. This line listens to you. What does it draw there? It's yours to decide."

CHAPTER 16

As she scrolled through one result after the next, Elaine's eyes were beginning to get tired. She searched and she searched through image after image of the desert landscape and terrain. Trying in vain to try and find some sort of clue or a hint as to what happened to Leila. She was hoping beyond the shadow of a doubt that something would jump out at her. She tried to think like someone else because thinking like her normal self was not helping one bit.

Elaine looked at every angle of each photo. She even went and sat in a different part of the office to see if maybe a new direction of light or a different sound from what she normally heard would somehow ignite a new part of her brain.

As she continued to scroll and scroll through different images on her laptop, she began to give up hope. She began to get tired, and her eyes felt heavy. She picked up her laptop and went back into her office grabbing a cup of coffee on her way. As she got comfortable, she was suddenly startled by the heavy banging on the window that separated her office from Eric's.

The knock was coming from Eric's side, and it was him motioning her to come to his desk.

"What's up?" she asked.

"Get your things. We're going downtown," Eric ordered.

"Why?"

"There is a group of people I want to interview. Some Middle Eastern families who may be able to shed some light on what's going on here."

With the pendant in his hand, Eric put on his coat and motioned to Elaine to do the same.

Their car came to a stop outside the Coptic Orthodox Church and neighboring bakery in downtown Providence.

For more than 100 years, Providence has been home to Middle Eastern families. During the peak of the textile boom of the late 19th and early 20th centuries, Rhode Island was a beacon of hope for many Syrian, Lebanese, and Egyptian immigrants looking for work and fortune in America. Since then, Middle Eastern families have continued to gravitate to this part of New England with the same hopes and dreams as their forefathers. For a time, Rhode Island had been the destination for many refugees from this same part of the world, as they started new lives for themselves after escaping their war-torn homelands. Whether the family has been in Providence for more than a century, or whether the family is newly arrived, they all share the same trait that has drawn Eric to exploring this part of town: they all continue to hold the traditions, culture, and language of their homelands alive. If anyone can shed some light on Leila, how she came to arrive in the US, and what could have possibly happened to her, it would be her own people.

Eric and Elaine entered St. Mary Coptic Church through the huge open corridor leading to the front doors of the church. The modern mid-century architecture of the church seemed almost terrifying, yet it had a regal, strong feel that emanated strength and faith.

Upon entering the church, Eric and Elaine spotted the kneeling figure of Father John. The church was so quiet, Elaine could almost hear the dust settling on the pews. The large mural running around the circumference of the round room depicting the 12 Stations of the Cross sent chills through Elaine's body. The level of piety and cleanliness made her feel a sinner and a secular zealot.

As Eric and Elaine approached Father John, Eric motioned for the two of them to find a pew and take a seat, but before either one could make a move, Father John spoke. "Hello, my friends. I will be with you in just one second."

Almost startled, Elaine and Eric dared not move a muscle. Father John crossed himself, "In the name of the Father, and of the Son, and of the Holy Spirit. Amen." Father John rose, turned, and greeted his guests.

At first glance, Father John seemed almost frightening, yet devilishly handsome. A young man of maybe only his early 40s, Father John had wavy black hair that was just ever so slightly beginning to gray at the temples. His skin was olive, yet had a pale hue to it as from the many years in New England where summer is not eternal like his homeland. His eyes were black with long, black eyelashes that gave his eyes a shine that captured Elaine's attention immediately. His well-defined nose and full lips with his chiseled features and chin made it almost a shame that he was a man of the cloth.

"I apologize that you have caught me in the midst of prayer. I am usually done with my prayers by this time, but I was held up this morning by pressing church matters," Father John explained. "However, here we are and what can I do for you?"

Father John motioned for the two detectives to take a seat in the first pew. The huge altar with the domineering crucifix gave Eric a slight chill as if Jesus' harrowing, suffering eyes were calling upon him to solve this heinous crime.

As the three sat, Eric immediately began to conduct business. "Father, as I explained on the phone, we unfortunately found a young girl murdered. She was all of maybe 16 or 17 years old, and on her body we found this pendant."

Eric showed the pendant to Father John who carefully looked it over. After about a minute of scrutiny, he spoke. "I must admit that some of these symbols you describe do look familiar, but they are not indigenous of my particular area of Middle Eastern culture; therefore, my help will be limited. These signs are also more towards the Islamic faith than the Christian faith."

"I'm sorry, Father," Elaine said, "but could you clarify that for me."

"Of course, my people are Coptic. We are a sect of the Coptic Orthodox Christian Church that was formed hundreds of years ago as part of the Church of the East in Egypt. I am personally of Egyptian heritage, although both my parents and I were born here. Our church's headquarters are in Alexandria. It has been there for many years."

"I see," Elaine said.

"Is there anything that you can tell us about these symbols, Father?" Eric asked.

"Well, I am not a master of symbols, detective, but at first glance the tree is similar to trees back in the Middle East. I am second-generation American, so I have never actually been to the Middle East, but I do notice this type of tree from family photos taken from when my grandparents lived there."

"Yeah. We kind of learned that already. We were hoping that maybe you could shed some more of a cultural aspect on this," Eric asked with some urgency in his voice.

"Well," Father John said with some hesitation as he looked at it some more. He furrowed his brow and then looked down at the pendant before turning it over in his hand and clenching it in his fist. "There may be one connection I can see here, but I don't think I would be your expert in this endeavor."

"We'll take any lead at this point, Father," Elaine said with a slight blaze in her eyes.

"Well, this pendant and this tree may be symbols of a nomadic culture that has its origins in the Middle East, but has mostly settled in the Sinai Peninsula."

"What culture would that be, Father?" Eric asked, moving forward in his seat.

"It would be the Bedouin Culture. Iraq has an area where these tribes live, as do Jordan, Syria, and Egypt. I believe once you pass the Sinai Peninsula, the tribes reach across Egypt and as far west as Morocco and as far south as Sudan. This tree could be one of their symbols. I am not a tree expert, but I believe that these trees are also found in Africa, so it would make sense."

"We've been told something similar already, Father. Do you know of anyone who can shed more light here?" Eric asked.

"I can ask a friend at the university where I sometimes teach classes on religious studies. There is a science department, but if you are looking for answers right away, perhaps you should go next door to the bakery owned by an Egyptian family that has been here for almost 70 years. They may know more since their eldest member actually lived in the Middle East.

Elaine bolted up. "Thank you Father, we will go right away."

"Again, I wish I could have been of more help, but if you have any religious questions, I am always here to help."

"Thank you for everything, Father," Eric said.

"You're welcome."

Eric and Elaine immediately left the church and headed right for the bakery a few doors down.

The inside of the bakery was bustling with customers who were buying sweet meat pies, fresh bread, and Middle Eastern cuisine. Eric was able to make his way through the throng of people and got the attention of the middle-aged woman working the register.

"Sorry, mister, but the line starts back by the front door. Order on your left, and once you have your food, you can pay me. Thanks, sir," she said and looked past Eric and Elaine. "I can help who's next and ready to pay?"

"Oh no, sorry, I am not a customer. I just have a quick question."

"Sorry, sir, but I'm a bit slammed right now and really can't answer any questions." The woman motioned a customer who pushed between Eric and Elaine to get to the register. "What do you have, hon? Three loaves of bread?"

Elaine, feeling the pressure of time running out as they searched for clues, reached into the inside pocket of her coat, produced her badge, and placed it right in front of the woman's face. The woman stopped what she was doing and simply looked Elaine in the eyes. Without withdrawing her gaze she called out, "Hey, Charlie, take the register for a few minutes. I have to show these extremely nice people into the back."

"Yeah, sure," mumbled a 17 year old who clearly felt he had better things to do.

The woman showed the two detectives into the back room of the bakery that was set up to look like a small apartment that housed a kitchen area with refrigerator, couch, TV, kitchen table, and chairs. The kitchen table looked like something out of the late 20th century with a plastic tablecloth and lazy Susan in the middle of the table adorned with salt and pepper shakers, napkins, and a bottle of hot sauce. Over the stove and over the mid-century Formica cabinets and countertops were pictures of Jesus and the Virgin Mary. Eric and Elaine took in every aspect of the room from the linoleum flooring to the yellow valances hanging over the windows, to the ancient microwave on a white cabinet by the backdoor with a magnetic calendar on it given by Father John's church. The two almost felt transported back in time.

"Have a seat, officers," the woman said.

Elaine responded, "Detectives."

"I'm sorry?" the woman answered.

"We're detectives not officers."

"Oh. My apologies."

"Everyone around here seems to apologize," Elaine said with a note of annoyance.

Eric spoke first, "I'm sorry, we didn't get your name."

"Sara."

"Sara, nice to meet you," Eric said.

Sara looked at Elaine who said nothing.

Sara spoke next, "What can I help you with today?"

"Sara, were you born in Egypt?"

"That's a random question, detectives. If I may be so bold, I would like to remind you that you are in a Lebanese bakery."

The detectives looked at each other, and Eric gave Elaine a stern look. Elaine spoke next.

"Our turn to apologize. We assumed wrong."

"It's okay. Most of the Arabs in this city are either from Egypt, Syria, or Lebanon, so it's to be expected. No worries. But to answer your question, no, I was not born in Egypt. I was born here. My mother, however, was born in Alexandria in Egypt. It's my father who was Lebanese and started this bakery. Why is that helpful to you, detectives?"

"I don't know if you read the news lately, but a young teenage girl was found dead the other day. We believe she may be of Middle Eastern descent, and we also believe that some cultural aspects of where she comes from may be of some help to solving the investigation," Eric clarified.

"And what aspects are those?"

Elaine said, "Symbols of a possible nomadic culture that is found in that part of the world."

"The Bedouins?" Sara queried.

"Why yes," Eric said. "What can you tell us about them?"

"Not much. My uncle used to talk about how they would run tours for tourists and help them to navigate the desert and take them on excursions. My uncle always said that the Bedouins were so good at figuring out a desolate place like the desert that they could find their way around any place in the world."

"What else did your uncle say about these people?" Elaine asked.

"I really couldn't tell you. I was so young when he shared those stories."

"Where is your uncle now?" Eric asked.

"He passed away a few years ago from pneumonia. My mother, however, is the person you want to talk to. She remembers a lot for a woman who is almost 80 years old."

Eric stepped forward. "Where can we find her?"

Sara pointed behind Eric to a set stairs. "Right that way."

Sara took Eric and Elaine up a flight of stairs to an apartment above the bakery. The apartment had wood paneling, white lace curtains, a sofa dating back to the early '90s, and religious statues and portraits on almost every surface. Upon entering the living room area, Eric and Elaine were greeted by an elderly woman watching game shows from a recliner. On a small table next to the chair were a few bottles of prescription pills, tissues, magazines, and the photo of a young, handsome man that seemed to have been taken in the late '50s or early '60s. They quickly surmised that this photo was of Sara's father.

"Mama, there are some people here who want to talk to you."

"Oh, hello. How can I help you?" Sara's mother asked.

Elaine began, "Hello, I'm Detective Hernandez and this is Detective Gutenheim, and we just wanted to ask you some questions about your culture, if that's all right."

"Of course it is. I would love to help you as best as I can," the old woman said.

Elaine continued, "Perfect. Thank you very much. I guess to start, have you ever seen symbols like these?" Elaine showed the old woman the pendant. The old woman took the pendant in her fragile hands and put on a pair of glasses she pulled from her sweater pocket and began to look it over.

"Ah yes. This tree is a symbol of life. You can find trees like this all over the desert. The native peoples believe tree is like air. You must have tree to live. Sometimes people think that the desert is a place of death; however, there is much life in the desert. I was raised in Cairo, and there was much life happening there. Perhaps too much, which is why things are the way they are now, but I missed it when I moved here. But, raising a family and having a business made me forget..."

Eric spoke up, "Is there anything else you can see in the pendant?"

"I'm sorry, my dear," the old woman said, "but my eyes are not what they used to be."

"Of course," Elaine said. "We had the opportunity to inspect the pendant closer under a magnifying glass and there are more symbols there. There are several wedding symbols. Swords and headbands and such. Our expert said that it has something to do with the Al-Miiarkh tribe. We were wondering if you knew anything else about these symbols or about the tribe.

"I wish my brother was still here," said the old woman. "He

loved to research and talk about the Bedouin tribes. He was such a fanatic. It was a hobby of his to know everything about our ancient culture.

"When we were kids, he would go out into the desert a little way and try to spend time with the tribesmen and learn their ways. My brother thought it was such an amazing thing to be able to live in the desert and know the way around a place that varied very little. If he was here, my brother would be able to answer all of these questions."

Elaine asked, "So you have heard of these tribes. That's good. Is there anything he ever told you that you may remember? Anything about the tribes?"

The old woman took a moment to think. As she did, she seemed to get lost in a series of photos that were framed on her windowsill. Eric and Elaine waited patiently for an answer. Eventually, Sara spoke first, "Ma. Do you remember anything?"

"Oh, I'm sorry, dears," said the old woman as she looked at the photo of the young man on her side table.

"Mama, I don't think the answer is in Baba's photo," Sara said softly.

"Did you say the Al-Miiarkh tribe?" the old woman asked.

Eric's face lit up. "Yes. Yes we did."

"I was lost in thought trying to remember exactly. You know, we are Coptic Christians, but not all Bedouins are Muslims; some tribes are Christians, some are Muslims, and some are mixed. But we all live together, so it doesn't really matter. But there is something important you should know. Pendants like these were given as gifts and jewelry and are buried with the dead. It's like in the olden traditional days when Egyptian kings and queens were buried with their jewelries. It's an honorable thing to do. Honor is very important to these tribes. Family honor especially. Women in these tribes are like property. A man could kill his wife free of guilt or crime if she does not honor him."

All of a sudden, Eric stood up. His eyes got wide and his face got red.

"What is it?" Elaine asked.

"Nothing," Eric said as he looked at the old woman. "Thank you so much. You have been a great help." He then turned to Sara saying, "I am sorry we interrupted your work day. We'll let you go, you must be busy."

Sara stood up, and after thanks and good-byes, the detectives returned to their car.

"That was quick," Elaine said. "What happened in there?"

"It's what the old woman said," Eric blurted. "Pendants like these are buried with the dead. That means Leila was killed by another member of her tribe."

"Wait, what?" Elaine said in a cloud of confusion.

"It's like what the old woman said, the tribes are all about honor, and if a woman dishonors her husband he can kill her. The pendant was left in accordance with honor and tradition. It's the killer's mark.

CHAPTER 17

On Sunday night there was an email waiting for me.

Dear Adam,

Hope all is well with you.

Can you meet me tomorrow at my office, after class; let's say around 3:00 p.m.? I want to talk to you about something that I hope will interest you.

Have a good night,

Meredith Blair

Meredith, our school principal, is a woman whom I admire and respect very much. She is honest and hard-working. It's been nearly 10 years since she was appointed to run our school, Benjamin High, where I teach literature and creative writing classes. The school serves nearly 1,400 students in grades 9 through 12. Recently we were ranked 3rd place in our county for students' academic excellence.

Meredith understands the teachers and staff. She began her career as a science teacher herself. Later, she decided that the management field was more appealing. She returned to college where she completed advanced studies in education administration and leadership. After two more years where she specialized as assistant high school principal, she joined the leadership staff at Benjamin High School.

Meredith is more than a leader. She's the first to arrive to the office and the last to lock its doors. With Meredith one can find a sympathetic ear and wise advice. If there's someone who always keeps a smile and positive approach, that would be Meredith.

Not only do we, the teachers, feel comfortable approaching her, but also our counseling and administrative staff as well as our students seek her guidance.

I had zero concerns about attending this meeting, as a matter of fact, I was intrigued.

The next morning I arrived to school at my usual time, 7:00 a.m. At 7:38 the first bell rang, signaling the students to go to their classrooms.

During the day I was busy and didn't have time to think about the meeting. The bell rang again at the end of the day, 2:35 p.m. Students rushed to their lockers and to the buses waiting to take them home. Ten minutes later, quiet returned except for a few students lingering in the hallways.

I started to prepare for the meeting. I straightened my shirt and took a quick selfie to make sure that nothing was stuck between my teeth.

My classroom is located at the end of the corridor on the second floor. The administration and the principal offices are located on the ground floor, about a three-minute walk.

Her office door was open. I knocked gently.

"May I come in?" I asked. Meredith was sitting at her desk working on the computer.

"Of course," she smiled when she saw me and stood up. We shook hands.

"How are you, Adam?" She led me to a comfortable seating area. Two single burgundy sofas were in one of the corner of the office. Next to the sofas stood a small round coffee table covered with a white tablecloth and a simple vase with fabric flowers.

"I'm well, thank you, and you?" I asked politely.

"Everything is fine. Busy you know. From sunrise 'til I can't see straight anymore." She laughed. "The usual stuff, you know."

I smiled. Sometimes it feels like the workday is never over, not only for us, the teachers, but for everyone else, too. The brain continues to think way after the work hours are over.

"I wanted to talk to you about *The Pencil Pro,*" she said.

I smiled. "You too?"

"Yes," she laughed. "I'm an enthusiastic follower of your Facebook page."

I knew that. I saw her profile picture among our followers.

"But I had the impression that you are actually one of the quieter participants," I said with a slight chuckle.

"True, I didn't respond or comment on any of the posts yet, but I have been reading them all. You'd be surprised to know how many things you can learn from social media."

Meredith, like many other educators, realized the advantage and the power of online resources. More than once she stated how much she supports the integration of computers and technology into our schools. At our last teachers' meeting she stated, "You just need to find and bring the technological opportunities to my attention, and leave the budget concerns up to me."

"How can I help?" I asked her as I settled in on the sofa.

"That's exactly what I wanted to talk to you about. Listen, we have a professional training day coming up in two weeks."

"Yes," I nodded, "I saw it on the calendar."

"I thought you may agree to present *The Pencil Pro* and your model supporting it, as the keynote opening lecture. It shouldn't be too long, about half an hour to 45 minutes, something like that."

Twice a year, Meredith gathers the entire school staff for a professional meeting. Nearly 140 people participate at those meetings, including the teaching and administrative staff, the school's instructional support team, and others.

"I must correct you," I said. "This is not just my model. We are four people leading this project, kind of an experiment."

"So how did you come up with the idea? I mean, I'm curious to hear how did it all get started."

"Oh, umm," I hesitated. How do I tell her that it all started with an idea thrown into the air at Andy's Bar next to a beer mug and alcohol vapor?

"I'm not exactly sure," I stammered. "It was...you know...just an experiment between friends, a bet how to get more breakthrough ideas...we never intended to open a Facebook page... it was just that people wanted to join and it was too much for a phone group chat."

"Sounds great!" said Meredith with enthusiasm. "That's exactly how the biggest innovations in world history were created, just as a challenge among friends."

"No, no, we are not at that level. The distance between us and the great inventors of history is like the distance between Shakespeare and Napoleon."

Meredith laughed.

"So, what do you say, dear Adam? Would you agree to stimulate us with your breakthrough ideas?"

This time I laughed out loud. "I'd love to," I replied. "I'll set up a presentation and some thinking exercises for the thirsty crowd. I just hope that the science teachers don't fall asleep."

"On the contrary," said Meredith. "When it comes to science subjects, there's much room for different thinking. Who said that two plus two always equals four? Maybe it's an event when chemical compounds melt one into the other and get infinite number of particles?"

"This is too much for me," I chuckled.

"Actually, at this time of the day, for me, too," she said followed by a giggle.

"Very well," she said escorting me to the door. "So, thank you, Adam, and a big "Like" to *The Pencil Pro*."

ഇരു

"For the opening lecture I would like to invite a special person." There was silence in the big school auditorium. Meredith stood on the stage in front of the silver microphone. The light was dim except for spotlights targeted at the stage.

"You all know Adam as well as I do. He always smiles, he's a dedicated teacher who's loved by his students, and he enjoys country music and Thai food." I could hear giggles in the audience.

"But there's something I doubt that you know about Adam. Adam Schwartz is not just a teacher. He has another expertise. Adam is a developer and challenger of the thinking. He develops keys to unlock your brain. Yes, until a few weeks ago, I had no idea what it means. I asked Adam Schwartz to join us today not only as part of our school's teaching staff, but also, as a guide and as the developer of *The Pencil Pro*. Today, Adam will teach us how to think differently. I encourage you to listen to his words and follow him on Facebook. Adam Schwartz, the stage is all yours."

Applause.

I left my chair and walked toward the stage. My knees were shaking. I felt a cold sweat sliding down my back. Standing in front of the class is one thing, but standing in front of 140 colleagues is quite intimidating.

I kept going and went up the stairs. My hands were locked on the pages I held. I felt the hard plastic of the USB stick that I had brought along as a backup in my pocket. I approached the silver microphone, which greeted me with a loud screech of feedback.

"I'm sorry," I said.

"Hello, friends, and thank you for inviting me to open the meeting today." The microphone worked. I heard my voice echoing in the hall.

"My name is Adam Schwartz, and I teach literature and creative writing in this school." The majority of our teachers know who I am since I've been working here for the past 11 years. However, with people who work at special positions, I don't have daily contact. I was not sure how many of them I knew by name and how many of them know me.

My hands were sweating. My heartbeat was as if I had just ran a marathon. My cheeks reddened. Truth be told, I was nervous. This rare opportunity to present and talk about our project along with the fact that I had some public speaking fear made me uncomfortable.

I stared at the auditorium while the spotlights dazzled me. My voice sounded through the sound system. I've never heard myself this way before. I was scared.

Nevertheless, with this opportunity that Meredith gave me, and its challenge to explain our project in front of a crowd of people, I was not ready to give up. I took a deep breath. I had memorized the speech for hours in front of the mirror. I prepared the PowerPoint presentation and prayed that everything would work out fine.

"I'd like to begin my talk today with a personal story. Many years ago, when my sister and I were young, we loved to play a card game that our mom got for us on one of her visits to Europe. It was a deck of cards that carried pictures from around the world. Next to each picture there were some sentences. Since both my sister and I had no idea what those sentences said, we tried to make up our own stories based on those pictures. This is how we played it: we placed a few cards each time on the floor in front of us, then each one got one chance to make up the best story related to the images. The most original story won points. I always believed that my sister had a wild imagination. She could free-associate the cards she got. She would make up stories about demons and elves and shipwrecks and pirates and many more things that popped into her head at that moment. When it was my turn to play the cards, I'd study the cards quietly. Then, I'd say a few sentences in a calm voice of what I thought happened before and after. I remember that even back then I thought there was a dichotomy in the world. Some people are more creative, and some people are not.

"It took me many years to realize that I was wrong."

I paused for a moment and then continued. "Creativity comes in many forms. You don't have to write a book or draw the best picture to show how creative you are. I'll give you an example. How many times were you standing in front of the half-empty fridge thinking what to make for dinner and then all of a sudden came up with a winning recipe? How many people here decided to re-organize their living room to 'give it another feel' and found it much more comfortable than what they had for years? How many people connected suddenly between two things and said to themselves: 'wow, this is genius!'" I heard whispers in the audience and nods of agreement.

"I would like to add one more thing to this list. It is called: 'the "Aha" moment'. "Aha" moments are the first spark of generating ideas and creativity.

"Think of the half-empty refrigerator example when you look at the half tomato, half onion, and a leftover pepper. Then, all of a sudden it hits you: "AHA!" I can still make pizza with those toppings for dinner.

"Aha" moments happen when our brain finally realizes something. It's a moment of inspiration or recognition; when we suddenly make a connection between two things or more, or when we process some information which all of a sudden makes sense. They can happen anytime and anywhere, when an apple falls on your head or when you soak in a bathtub.

"Remember 'a small spark can go a long way'." I paused. "Before I present our model, I'd like to ask you to remember two things: One: You cannot solve 21st century problems with 20th century solutions, meaning, a great solution you had yesterday might not work again tomorrow. Two: in order to be successful, you must generate original ideas. If you agree with both statements, then you're going to love our model. Our model can spark your brain and create those "aha" moments for you. We called our model *'Be Empowered with Creativity'* or by its popular name *'The Pencil Pro'*."

My voice trembled. I felt like I was putting out our model for a test. Will it work?

"Our model is based on three principles. The first key is to break the patterns. We are all locked in patterns. We love our daily routines. They make us comfortable and give us stability. We know what to do, how to act, and what's coming next. Our model asks you to break some of those patterns, though not all. You must break patterns in order to generate breakthrough ideas. If you follow our 24-hour exercise, we can teach you how to do that.

"Our second key principle asks you to make random connections. Yes, that's correct. Practice making up links between things that at first sight seem to have little or nothing in common. A smart guy made the connection between his computer and his cell phone. A lot of people laughed at him. They thought he was crazy. I'm not so sure they are laughing today. Again, our exercises can show you how to do that.

"And our third key and the most important principle, in my opinion, is to practice. Yes, think of your brain as any other muscle in your body. If you challenge, practice, and empower it, you'll be happy with its results.

"Our *'Be Empowered with Creativity'* model can help you do that. Look at the exercises we have posted on our Facebook page and practice them. Read a book but start from its ending. Look at situations from different perspectives. Ask "why" questions. Make up your own stories or make unexpected endings to various stories. Look for clues and hidden messages and so on. The most important thing I can tell you today is to practice. Practice, practice, and practice, so when it comes to real-life situations, your brain will find the creative solution needed.

"The Pencil Pro was launched several months ago. A few weeks ago we opened it up to our Facebook followers and friends. Currently we're being followed by nearly 15,000 people." People reacted with a "wow" and applause.

I looked at my watch. Wow! I couldn't believe that almost half an hour was already over. I didn't want to leave my talk today without letting the people get a feel for our model. But, there was something else I needed to say before I left the stage.

"There's one more thing I'll mention before moving on to the exercises. There's no doubt that younger children have a higher level of imagination. This is not a competition. Children are not afraid to express their minds. No one limits their imaginations. No one thinks they are crazy. They have not yet been told that things are impossible. The force of gravity will be learned with time. Currently they are children, and no one will convince them that a Lego spacecraft cannot fly. Try to think the same way. Don't let anything limit your imagination. Remember, be successful, be creative. I hope that the following exercises will help you see what I mean."

At the end of the Professional Day meeting, a few teachers approached me and shook my hand. "We heard about the project, but never imagined you were behind the scenes." We laughed. Nico tapped me firmly on my shoulders and said, "My daughter is 15 years old, and she follows you on Facebook. Finally, she learns something other than just teenager nonsense."

"Tell me something," Martha queried. "Those things that drive the network crazy, is that you, too? The dress that changes colors when you look at it from different angles?"

"No, that's not me." I was embarrassed. I felt like a child that passed the entrance exams to the popular team in school.

"So, what's next?" The question was thrown into the air. "What are you going to do with this project now?"

"I don't know. We didn't really think about it."

"Well, you can't hide behind the Facebook page forever," Nico suggested. "You have to spread the word outside. I'm sure that more people want to know about it. Maybe write a blog, publish a book, make a movie, God's know what. Just don't leave it like that hanging up in the air."

Chapter 18

From the darkest mind of a potential killer:

During the daytime I work intensively. I'm up at dawn, wash my face with cold water from the Bahla, our clay water pot that was drawn from the well. I clean the gravel from the largest pillows and carpet that are covering the floor of the tent. Then I take my time to light the fire. I drink some goat milk and eat pita bread.

When the sun begins to shine, it is time to take the goats to the pasture. They do not like to travel in the darkness.

They love it, the goats. They are bleating merrily. They enjoy their freedom.

The shepherds sometimes play music on a flute

made from a hollow tree branch. Beautiful sounds come out when fingers block the holes.

We love music here in our tribe. Sometimes we beat the drums or play the Rebab, a musical instrument with a long neck and two strings.

When the west wind blows, it is time to bring the goats back home.

During the herding, sometimes you may hear a jackal howling or a wolf growling. Shepherds were taught not to be afraid of predatory animals. Animals are sensitive to smell and if the shepherd is scared, they can smell the fear. You must never show them your fear. You must freeze and then back away slowly.

Shepherds can chase other animals and threaten them not to get closer. Shepherds can overcome the birds of prey and tear them up with their own bare hands. With the Sa'eif they cut off their heads first, then pluck them before stripping their skin and taking the meat back to the women's tent to be roasted for dinner

We are strong people, here in our tribe. We are not afraid. Our fathers taught us that we must be strong. A man who is scared is a man who is cursed by the gods, and that's a big problem because even his own sons will be cursed – just like him. No beasts or wild animals can scare us.

But...there's one thing...one thing that I don't like... It is the darkness.

As soon as darkness takes over, I feel surrounded by evil spirits that come from nowhere, and it feels like being twisted and tossed to and fro.

It begins with the devilish laughter tearing the darkness. It feels like falling into a deep abyss. You want to get up, but you can't.

Cool breeze is blowing. It plays with a black veil, tousling the hair. I chuckle. Put my hand up to cover my mouth. Delicate fingers, shiny skin. But the veil takes on a life of its own. It rises upward and breaks loose. It gently flies over the head, and its ends are caressing me, just touching the cheeks. I chuckle again. How beautiful it is! How gentle it is, like I never lived in this arid desert. Then, suddenly the veil stands erect and stops. The veil listens, sniffing around. It catches me watching it. The veil is laughing.

Now that laughter is not subtle. The veil is threatened and ready to attack. The smiles are melting away. Feet are planted in the ground. I try to pick up my feet and run. To find cover

from this veil that has gone insane. I'm stuck.
I can't run. My feet do not respond and this
veil is coming toward me to catch me, wanting
to tear me up. I start running, and the veil is
chasing me. It hits lightly, slaps at my head,
my face, inside my eyes. I keep running and
fall down deep into the dark abyss on a black
dress. I get up but fall down again, and the veil
goes up and up. Darkness. Absolute darkness. It
comes to cover me, to choke me, to smother and
tear my flesh.

Who are you and who are your masters? The
veil demands to know.

Voices wrap me softly and drown me in the gaze.
Pretty faces. Magical and dreamy eyes.

Can this veil bring us together or drive us
apart? Can you hear me? My heart is burning
for you.

Are you dreaming of a place, my love, far
away? A place where joy can be found?

We are both prisoners. You're helpless, just like
me.

Satan's bitter laughter. Ironical destiny. After
all, Jamal is the eldest brother. He has the
right. The sovereignty is his.

CHAPTER 19

The sound of an incoming text message woke me up. I grumbled. Saturday morning not even 7:00. Who's waking me up so early?

"Rob's in the hospital again. It's not good. We're at de Village."

I jumped out of bed, threw on my clothes, and rushed to the hospital.

"What happened?" I met Miriam in the corridor outside the recovery room.

The hospital *"de Village"* was located on the outskirts of the city. According to the number of beds and the percentage of the full-time medical staff, it is considered a small hospital.

Miriam led me to the waiting room next to the recovery room.

"His injury has become infected. He spiked a temperature of 103.5. The doctors took him into intensive care with IV antibiotics and cold towels to reduce the fever. It seems that the infection caused an irregular heartbeat. He looks very weak," she summarized it up for me.

"Poor guy," I whispered. "What can I do to help?"

Miriam didn't say anything. The worn-out sofa with the green cover creaked as she collapsed onto it. She burst into tears. "He is so weak and so helpless with all those tubes and monitors connected to his chest... My Rob... My silly guy... What will I do if I lose him?"

I hugged her, "I love you, sis. Everything will be fine. I promise," I whispered. "He's strong. He'll be just fine, you'll see," I said, my voice cracking.

Two hours later a Cardio-version consisting of stopping the heart and re-starting it was performed in order to re-establish a regular heartbeat. Atrial fibrillation is extremely dangerous to any patient. It has to be put under control as soon as possible.

Afterwards, I went to find the doctor in charge.

"The fever is still too high and it's slowing down the heart rate," he explained. "We have to closely monitor his heart rate and blood pressure."

At noon, I went to the cafeteria on the second floor and got us some coffee and a sandwich. "You must eat something," I pleaded with Miriam. We sat across from each other.

Miriam took a sip of the coffee. "I can't," she whispered. "To see the person you love so much, the tall strong guy with his warm heart, who just yesterday played with Lizzie and raised her on his shoulders and now, look at him, like that, lying in bed with all those monitors. It hurts so much."

"I know, sis," I almost cried with her, "but, please, you have to be strong for him, for yourself, for the kids." I tried to be optimistic. "Anything can happen in the next few hours, you know. He may recover and be back to bother us all with his new wooden models." Miriam tried to smile, but tears soon morphed the smile into a distraught grimace.

She whispered, "That's exactly right. Anything can happen in a few hours, if not in a few minutes."

Half an hour later the nurse came outside and asked Miriam to follow her. I heard soft crying rising from the hallway.

I called my parents.

"Nothing new yet," I told them. "No, Mom, there is no point for you to come here. It's a long journey." I listened to her plea. "Yes, I promise to keep you updated if anything changes. Yes, I'll tell Miriam. Love you. Bye for now." When I hung up, my head felt heavy with sorrow and apprehension.

I also called Miriam's and Rob's house to make sure that everything was under control. The babysitter answered the phone and assured me that everything was fine. It was the same babysitter who had been working with the kids for the last three years.

"The neighbor came over to check if we needed anything and if we heard any news from Miriam. She's worried. She saw the ambulance last night. She brought over a pot with spaghetti and meatballs for the kids." In the background I could hear the kids playing and having fun.

"That's very nice of her," I said. "Is everything all right there? I can hear the kids squealing in the background."

"Yes, everything is fine. It's a nice day today, and the kids asked to wear bathing suits and play in the garden. I hope it's okay."

"Yes, of course, it's fine," I assured her. "I'm sure they're having fun. I'll call later if there's news."

I hung up the phone.

Who could imagine that while the kids were having water fights, just a few blocks away their father was fighting for his life?

Several hours went by. It got dark outside. Miriam was still next to Rob's bed. This waiting was really nerve-wracking. I tried to flip through some magazines. I couldn't concentrate. I stood up and walked back and forth in the corridor. I looked through the large windows facing the side street to the backside of the hospital. Streetlights sent a pale yellowish light. I drew a circle with my finger in the condensation accumulated on the bottom of the window. Just like a child, I began to draw circles on the window. I drew small circles, curves, and random shapes.

It was almost 11:00 p.m. when the door finally opened and Miriam came out from the ICU looking exhausted.

"No, no change," she said. "They asked me to talk to him, to hold his hand. The medical team thinks that if he hears my voice or feels the warmth of my body it may help. In the meantime, nothing happened." She could barely keep her eyes open. I saw the despair, the anxiety, and the fear of the worst in those clouded eyes.

I hugged her. "I'm so sorry," I whispered. "If only there was something I could do to make it easier for you." I felt Miriam melting down in my arms. I wrapped my arms around her trying to comfort, to protect, to support her.

The big grandfather clock in the corner of the waiting room chimed midnight. A small metal golden plate was attached to the clock that read: *This clock was generously donated by the Henson family in memory of Greg Henson.*

It was an old, elegant clock, the casing of which was carved out of solid mahogany. The large pendulum turned the wheels and led the dials to their exact place. It gave the room a feeling of nostalgia and sober tranquility.

"A similar clock was at Nanna's and Papa's home, remember?" Miriam asked.

"Not really," I replied. "They passed away before I even turned six years old." Our parents found them embracing each other's arms sleeping the eternal rest.

"I remember their clocks. Papa loved clocks. He had a collection of them all over the house. I remember that the old grandfather clock made a strange noise, and grandpa used to tell me that if I listened very carefully I could hear what it was telling me. I remember I just thought that probably something was broken inside and needed to be fixed."

She glanced at the clock again. "Wow, it's very late. I talked with the kids earlier and wished them good night. They asked me to read a story for Daddy, but to start it from the ending." She gave me a sidelong glance, "Your idea, huh?"

I smiled.

"You have to go to bed too, my little brother," she added.

"I'm fine here," I lied. "The sofa is comfortable for a nap."

Miriam looked at the green sofa for a moment and smiled. "You really think you can fool me? Go home. Take a rest. I'll call you if there's anything new. It can take days, you know."

I sighed, "Okay, but promise you'll call if there's any change. No matter what. Anytime."

"I promise," she said walking me to the door then kissing me on the cheek . "Take care of yourself, you hear me? I don't know what I'll do if I lose you, too."

We hugged one more time and said goodbye.

It was 2 a.m. and I still rolled and tossed in bed. Sleep was far away from me.

The only question running through my head was: Why?

Why did it happen to Rob? Why all of a sudden did everything became entangled? Why can't the world just be good and happy? Why do we only appreciate life when it's too late?

Why is there suffering in the world? Why are some people hungry and sick? Why sometimes do we wake up in the morning with sudden pain and sometimes the pain is gone, but sometimes it stays with us?

Why is there no cure for all ailments? Why do certain drugs help some people but not others? Why are injections painful?

Why isn't the world just perfect?

The pendulum never swings in one direction. Pain and happiness have to keep order in the world.

Rob's condition improved. It took about 10 more days before he was released from the hospital. He was given precise guidelines and antibiotics that filled his medicine cabinet. He promised the doctors to be obedient, change bandages on time, and not tempt fate.

Rob learned his lesson, as did those who were close to him. Miriam hired another assistant at the clinic and took two weeks off just to spend time with her family. Rob cut down the time he devoted to his woodcarving in favor of his health.

And as for me, I never went back to taking life for granted.

80C3

Although it was only my second time recording a YouTube clip, I felt more confident.

The technical part of recording and uploading the file to my library on YouTube was pretty simple, and my first video clip garnered some interests and accumulated some "likes." Johnny was right. I can understand why this method of communication works out better for my students. They get to see my face and hear my voice while I enjoy the comfort of my living room.

I sat back and took a deep breath. I was ready. I clicked on the recording button.

"When I was in third grade," I began talking, while looking straight at the camera, "Ms. Baker, our math teacher, raised the following question:

'Who knows how much is five plus three?' She even wrote it on the board like this: 5 + 3 =

"We were happy. That was an easy exercise. We knew that the answer was the number eight = 8

"Then the teacher 'tricked' us and erased the numbers 5 and 3 and the plus sign. She left on the board only: = 8

"'And now?' she asked, 'Who can tell me what's equal to 8?'

"The answer was an endless series of possibilities when you are using addition, subtraction, multiplication, division, positive or negative numbers, decimals, and more.

"'You see, children?' she said finally, adding, 'It all depends on how you ask the question.'"

People have always been taught to ask questions. Parents have learned that there's a normal developing childhood stage when children repeat the question "why" endlessly. Kids become curious and want to learn and acquire knowledge. They want to link "cause" and "effect," or better, to understand complex phenomena.

People use questions all the time. Questions are important. They help us understand. They provide a solution to our natural curiosity. They help us collect information. They give us "answers" to emotional goals and much, much more.

When we are asked questions, we feel important, loved, respected, and wanted.

Asking questions in general, and in particular the "why" question, provokes our thoughts. I understand the fact or argument that was presented in class (What Equals 8), but I don't necessarily accept it as it is (is it just 3 + 5? Are there no other options?) Basically, by asking "why" we inquire as to what was the idea, the circumstances, or processes that lead to a conclusion or to the facts involved.

Research suggests that people who ask more questions succeed more in life. That's a fact. The question is: why?

The answer is simple: curiosity. The leaders and the best entrepreneurs never stop thinking and exploring the world. They do not accept reality as it is presented to them. Nothing is taken for granted. They want to know more, to challenge the conventions. They see their environment as a source of knowledge and are thirsty for it.

People who ask understand that sometimes you have to rephrase the question in a different way to get a different answer.

Let's try it out.

Exercise No. 7

Questions

Read the following story:

It was a cold night. I was on my way home from work. I was tired and a little hungry. The girl that was supposed to take over my shift was an hour late.

It was about 10:15 p.m. when I stopped at the gas station. I remember the time because I looked at my watch before I left the car. The parking lot was empty and quite dark, but it was the only shop still open.

I went straight to the refrigerator and took out a bottle of milk. On the way I collected a loaf of sliced bread wrapped in a plastic bag. I went over to the cashier. I remember him. I think he was a guy in his 40s, short black hair, shorter than me. I don't remember his eyes because he kept looking down. He quickly scanned the groceries. The total was $7.75.

"And I'd like a pack of cigarettes," I said.

"What kind?" he asked, still not looking up.

"Marlboro Lights."

He hesitated for a moment, and then he went to get it. He seemed a bit nervous. I thought he was tired, probably couldn't wait to lock up and go home. He returned to the cash register and scanned again.

"$15.23," he said.

I gave him a $20 bill. He gave me change without looking

up. I said goodnight and left. The next morning I saw the following item in the newspaper: "A man, 42 years old, was killed last night in a store next to the PZ gas station. He was stabbed with a knife. The killer was hiding under the cashier's counter for over an hour, waiting for the store to be empty."

Your Mission: Try to come up with at least 10 questions you can ask about this story. Start with one question and see where it leads you.

Try to see the story from various perspectives: the investigator who came to the murder scene, the main suspect or the witness at the police station, the victim's thoughts prior to his death, or perhaps even the killer who was hiding.

Try to be original; perhaps there was another person who could testify and shed some light on what happened; perhaps another figure like the killer's mom or another person? Let your mind wander and imagination flow with the story.

Also, you may ask theoretical questions with no clear answer. This may be an unanswered existentialist question.

This is not an easy task, so don't be afraid to try a few times.

Remember, the word **"why"** must appear in each and every question at the beginning, middle, or end of the sentence.

CHAPTER 20

As Eric and Elaine emerged from their vehicle at the top of the hill, a slight chill crept down Eric's spine. This was the place where the body had been found. This is the place where he first recognized the feeling that everything was not even close to what it appeared to be.

The two detectives walked down the path leading to the bridge and the crime scene. As Eric walked along the path with Elaine behind him, he took in every aspect of the park. Every bench, every dog barking at birds, every blade of grass did not go unnoticed.

The path wound through the grassy knoll and ended at the dirt that bordered the river. Eric and Elaine walked over the cold dirt and under the bridge.

When the two arrived, the dirt was still slightly out of place where the paramedics had brought in the gurney.

In that moment, Eric remembered the ripped up pieces of

paper that were found with the symbols on them. Eric stopped and looked out at the river, and while he was reflecting, he quickly reached into the inner pocket of his jacket and retrieved the taped up pieces. The weird symbols that when looked at made no sense or seemed to be in no particular order.

As Eric walked around the area, he and Elaine tried to figure out what would have brought Leila to this spot, to a place that was outside of her normal routine. A place that would be the last spot she would ever stand on this Earth.

"I don't get it," Elaine said frankly. "Why come down here? Why this spot?"

"I think that's the first place we need to start," Eric responded. "Maybe if we can figure out why here then maybe all the other pieces will come together."

The two detectives wandered back towards the path retracing Leila's steps bit by bit.

"Okay," Elaine spoke first, "what if she ran into someone on a previous day, or someone at work? Maybe she had an impromptu rendezvous?"

"That's not a bad idea," Eric agreed, "but who would she have run into cleaning a restaurant overnight?"

"That's true," said Elaine, lowering her eyes while searching the ground for anything that might give them a clue.

They stood there another moment in silence.

"Okay," Eric finally said after a few moments. "In what

direction would she have entered the park?"

"If she came here from work, then that would have been the northeast entrance to the park."

"Okay. Perfect. We'll start there. Let's say she entered the northeast entrance and then walked along the sidewalk along the car path. That means she would have come onto the path right where we parked," Eric assumed.

Elaine responded, "Right. Then she would have entered the path from where the car is, and she would have taken the most direct path. If you are going to meet someone, then you are not going to dawdle. She would have come down along the left side to the other side of the bridge."

"Do me a favor, Elaine," Eric said. "I'm going to stand here on the spot where she was killed, and you take Leila's path."

"Done."

Elaine then hurriedly walked across the grass to the path that led up to the car. As Eric stood in the spot, he watched Elaine briskly take the path that was assumed to be Leila's last walk of her life, around the entrance to the bridge to come underneath it, stopping right in front of Eric.

"Now what?" she asked.

"Something is missing, Elaine. If I was expecting you I would be facing you, but it seems as if she was murdered from someone that came from behind her. Why would she take this direct and deliberate path to this very spot if she wasn't coming for one specific reason or another?" Eric posed a lot for Elaine to think about.

"What was her reason for coming to this very deliberate spot?"

"Let's think again about what was found," Elaine reasoned. "Her identification, which was clearly fake. The pendant, which is indicative of her real culture, and that ripped up piece of paper."

"Okay," Eric came to life. "Why was the paper ripped up? Was it the killer who ripped it up, or was Leila ripping it up and going to the garbage can just 15 feet away?"

Elaine's eyes got large. "Maybe she found it in her pocket or on the ground and decided to throw it away and someone came out of nowhere to kill her?"

"As much sense as that makes, everything was planted far too well for it to be a random act of violence," Eric retorted.

"Right." Elaine seemed disappointed. "Perhaps the message was given to her by whomever she was meeting and whatever it means angered her and she ripped it up and the other person killed her during the altercation?"

"There were no signs of struggle. One thing is clear," Eric said, "this was a deliberate act, and Leila's final facial expression had peace written all over it."

The two detectives spent the next half hour going over and over Leila's final steps, but nothing in the park or at the crime scene could reveal any clues or any other information that could prove helpful. Eric went into one of the outer pockets of his blazer and pulled out the pendant. He kept thinking, why was everything placed in such a way?

"We have to decipher these symbols," Eric said as he

produced the taped up card from his pocket. "There is something about them that does not meet the eye."

"They seem to not mean much of anything, to be honest," Elaine said. "They simply seem to be a drawing that Louisa made, if anything ."

Immediately, Eric perked up. His eyes began searching the park as if he realized that he was missing something, something important. "What entrance did we enter the park?" he asked Elaine.

"The northeastern entrance. Why?"

"Come on," Eric said and began to walk across the grass instead of the path, making a direct line for the top of the hill. Elaine followed behind him as fast as she could to keep up with him.

Eric walked past their car and kept walking along the car path, walking so fast that he took to walking in the street to avoid having to dart around slow walking people. Eventually, Eric made his way to a playground just short of the north entrance. Eric stopped when he approached the playground. Elaine met up with him and stopped to catch her breath from the fast walk.

"Why are we here?" she managed to ask through large inhales.

"Here, he was here," Eric said with confidence.

Elaine was more than confused. "Who was here, Eric?"

"The Green Ghost," Eric said with a broad smile on his face. "The guy that scared Louisa. This is the playground her foster parents took her to when she said that she saw the Green Ghost in the bushes."

"Wait, what are you driving at, Eric?"

"Leila knew her killer. And her killer is the Green Ghost. If he was here when Louisa was here, it was because he frequented this spot. He either knew she would be here, or he is always here and by coincidence saw Louisa the other day, which is why they were both a bit caught off guard. It had to be a coincidence because otherwise he wouldn't have tried to approach her so abruptly. Leila knew her killer. That's why there was no struggle. That's why her expression was peaceful. There was no arguing. There was no altercation. This was planned. That's why everything was planted. It was a sacrifice. It was an offering to the gods, but why? What does it all mean?"

"That's a lot of circumstantial thinking, Eric," reasoned Elaine. "Chances are this was random. There is no way to prove that the Green Ghost was here and she knew it. Maybe just like Louisa, he didn't expect to see Leila, and while she was simply enjoying the view down by the river, he came up behind her and slit her throat?"

Eric's face dropped. He knew Elaine was right. There was no way to prove that his idea was indeed watertight. Eric exhaled deeply and ran his fingers through his hair. He was once again stumped. He and Elaine were still at square one.

"Don't be let down," Elaine said trying to soothe Eric. "Your ideas have done one thing for us, we are starting to see things differently. Something that we are used to seeing one way has truly several meanings. This is good."

"Yeah, but the only thing about this whole affair is that

everything seems pretty black and white. We are just missing a few obvious pieces. Pieces that we may never find. It's been a few days, Elaine, I'm afraid this case is going cold, and I am even more afraid that I am letting Louisa down. Her mother was ripped away from her, and there is nothing I can do about it."

"Hey, don't put this kind of pressure on yourself, Eric. You are doing a great job, and maybe this isn't as simple as we think it is. I mean, we've gone from dead bodies and little girls to hieroglyphics. We've kind of run the gamut here."

"Hieroglyphics. That's it. Elaine, that's it!" Eric exclaimed rushing back to the car. Elaine quickly ran after Eric wondering where they were off to next.

Back at the station, Eric threw his coat on the couch in his office and slammed himself into the chair at his desk. He started up his computer and began to do an Internet search. He took the taped up pieces of paper with the symbols on it and put it on this desk on top of the myriad other papers and sticky notes.

Elaine, after tossing her own jacket into her office, went into Eric's office and stood behind him as he searched the Internet.

"What are you looking for?" she asked. "We were in the middle of being defeated, and all of a sudden you were off."

"You said hieroglyphics. That got me thinking, what if these weird symbols are more symbols from the Bedouin tribe? What if they are some way of communicating that is ancient or something?"

"Interesting," Elaine was impressed. "Very interesting. Let's see what you come up with."

Eric began to search Bedouin symbols, but he kept getting Egyptian hieroglyphics. "I know the Bedouins live in Egypt, but is everything Egyptian hieroglyphics?" Eric was getting antsy. He eventually stopped and just stared at the screen revealing nothing.

"Well, was Leila's tribe Egyptian?" Elaine asked.

"I don't think we ever found out where exactly she was from," Eric said. "Maybe the Kalahari? That's in Africa. It's just south of Egypt."

"Well, perhaps she was from there and these symbols are Egyptian."

"Clearly, they are not," Eric was getting angry. "Or else they would match our search."

"Well the tribes are nomadic, aren't they? Perhaps certain symbols are retained and lost in translation so to speak?" Elaine began to brainstorm, saying, "Maybe we just need to look at it differently?"

"Wait a minute," Eric got excited again. "Look at this." Eric pointed to a symbol on the screen that closely resembled one on the ripped up card. "That Egyptian symbol for reed shelter. Look. It almost looks like that square."

"You're right," Elaine said. "Do any of the other symbols match up?"

Before long, the two detectives began picking out hieroglyphics that closely matched the weird symbols on the paper, and before long, a story seemed to emerge.

"Well," said Elaine, "some of these symbols make sense, but

others don't; however, the ones that don't might stand for something else."

"I think you're right. If you were to look at the first symbol what do you see?"

"Pac-Man," Elaine said.

"I doubt Pac-Man has anything to do with this," Eric said. "To me it looks like a three-quarter moon."

Elaine looked out the window and caught sight of the moon in the sky. It was almost full.

"Wait a minute," Elaine said walking to the wall calendar hanging on the opposite wall of Eric's desk, "what was the moon like on the day Leila died?"

Elaine searched the day of Leila's death of the moon symbol in the corner. Nothing. But on the following day, the symbol showed a moon at three-quarters full.

"It's directions," Elaine blurted out rushing back to Eric's desk and grabbing the taped up symbols. "They are plans. Well-laid plans. The first symbol is a three-quarter moon. That's the date, the second symbol by the hieroglyphics is a water ripple, that's the river. The third is kind of hard, it looks like a basket with a handle I don't know what that means."

"Or it could be directional, the arrow indicates going under something," said Eric.

"Like a bridge!" Elaine said excitedly.

"What about the next one?"

"A reed shelter or a stool. Maybe that means a meeting place.

A place to rest."

"Next?"

"Hieroglyphics: slope of a hill, that's where the bridge is," Elaine had more excitement in her voice.

"Next."

"It could either be a leg, a folded cloth, or maybe a corner."

"Keep going," Eric said.

"An hour glass, perhaps that means a certain time? Then an arrow, which could be the dagger, a thought cloud, and a do not enter symbol."

The two sat in silence.

"This means nothing," Elaine said, "It's a dead end."

Eric's eyes lit up. "No it's not. It's half-modern symbols and half-ancient symbols. It is a plan. You were right, Elaine, put it all together and use your imagination. Look: 'On the day of three-quarter moon, by the river, go under the bridge and wait at the bottom of the hill by the corner of the bridge. That's the time to use the dagger. Think. Death.'"

Elaine looked at Eric for a moment and then said, "She knew her killer."

"The Green Ghost?" Eric said.

"The Green Ghost," Elaine echoed.

CHAPTER 21

My students were enthusiastic about the story, as if they were real detectives in a kid's game.

"Why didn't the cashier call for help?" was the common question in class.

"Why didn't he write behind the receipt to call the police or someone else?"

"Why didn't the cashier try to engage the customer in a conversation and imply that he was in trouble?"

"Try again," I said. "These are very good questions, but common. Try to be more original than that."

"Okay. Why do we have to believe the testimony of the customer and not suspect that he was part of the plot?" someone tried to argue.

"Good. Very good. That's the direction I'm looking for. Don't accept the story as is. Keep thinking."

"Why didn't the customer stay at the store longer if he suspected that something was wrong?"

"Great. More ideas!" I was excited. The students warmed up. I could feel the wheels turning in their heads. They were looking for evidence, questions that had not been asked yet.

When someone tried to throw out a question that didn't have the word "why," they stopped themselves. There was a lot of babbling, squeaks, words like "how can you...", "who said that..?" which were left hanging in the air. The students were far from giving up. Their eyes were shining. Their brains worked overtime.

"Why was the murder carried out precisely in this way, with a knife? Were there no other alternatives?"

"Why rely on one piece of evidence? Why not look for other witnesses?"

"As the customer, why didn't the killer try to hurt me first?"

"As the killer, why wait an hour? Why not kill the cashier and the customer—two birds with one stone?"

"Why didn't the Universe intervene and prevent the murder or at least give us a sign that something bad was about to happen?"

"Good! I love your questions. Anyone else?" I said.

There was silence in the classroom. The students tuned out. Some just laid their head on the table and gave up. "I take it that you don't want to be police detectives," I said.

Then, my bright philosophical student Jen raised her hand, and, in a deep voice, asked, "Why is there evil in the world? Why do we believe in evil? The belief in evil is like we empower its needs, make evil flourish. By doing that we give it strength and actually legitimize it. Right?"

ಬಿೞಲ

By evening, our Facebook page was flooded with Why questions:

"Why is the world full of hatred?"

"Why not let the forces of the Universe (the cashier) get a second chance?"

"Why does it take a lifetime to search for the meaning of life?"

"Why do people expect the random world to be fair?"

"Why do we always judge others by their actions? Why do we give people titles, like "the cashier" or "the killer"?

"Why is there a dichotomy between weak and strong, good and evil, right and wrong, real and imaginary?"

"Why is there no warning before death?"

"Why do stories of crime appear in the headlines and of success in the secondary section?"

Drew and Cheryl also shared their own comments: "Why, when fear dominates us, do we become paralyzed and stop thinking?"

CHAPTER 22

Eric and Elaine stood in front of 23 Hope Street. *It's ironic,* Eric thought. *Hope is the one thing Leila didn't have but needed.*

"Where do we start?" Elaine asked. The two detectives looked around the neighborhood. Everything seemed to be serene and in place. Joggers passed by, people walked their dogs, kids were on their way to school, nothing out of the ordinary was happening. Just another regular day in the neighborhood. Isn't that how it always happens? The worst things in the world happen on the most ordinary of days.

"Well, I guess we should start at the beginning," Eric said as he pulled a piece of paper out of the inside pocket of his blazer. He unfolded the paper which was a list of places that Leila normally visited daily. Eric and Elaine decided that they would start at Leila's apartment on Hope Street. They would take the route that she normally took to work. The old Chinese lady was helpful in marking the path to the restaurant from Leila's apartment. It is a restaurant that she herself frequented, as it belonged to her family. From the restaurant, Eric and Elaine would then check the usual places the old Chinese lady said that Leila frequented when she ran errands (a grocery store down the street from the restaurant, a pharmacy where she sometimes pick up candy for Louisa), and finally the park, which although it was not on the normal route that Leila would take, she did take on the day she died . Eric and Elaine were able to rule out any bars or other crowded dining establishments as Leila was not old enough to have frequented these places, even with her fake ID, and also because they were not a typical part of her culture.

"Where does a 16 year old go during the day?" Elaine asked Eric as they walked down Hope Street in the direction of the restaurant.

"It's been so long since I was 16, I don't actually remember."

"I remember," Elaine said. "I used to hop on my bike and head down to the corner where my cousin Maria lived. All the kids would be hanging out in front of her building. My aunt divorced her husband when Maria and I were little, and he went back to Mexico. So my Tia Alma, Maria, and my other cousin Jorge were with us all the time."

"You lived on the same street?" Eric asked.

"Yeah, except we lived in a house. My mom and dad worked so hard for that house. I think that's why I feel so connected to

Leila. I see a young girl doing everything in her power to raise her kid. It reminds me of my own parents. My dad worked in a construction site, my mom worked long shifts at the hospital—it's all the same."

"That's the thing with cultures, Elaine, they are all the same." Eric began to get lost in thought. "That's what I have learned from being in New York. The dress, the language, and the religion might be different, but people are people no matter what. We all have the same problems, the same goals, and the same weaknesses. Just like your uncle who went back to Mexico."

"Yeah, he was kind of a deadbeat. He liked to drink a lot, and liked his family less. I don't think anyone in my family was the least bit sad when he decided to go back home."

"Did you guys ever see him again?"

"Once we took a family vacation back to Guadalajara, and we saw him, but he was unrecognizable by that time. His hard lifestyle and lack of responsibilities really did a number on him."

"Sorry."

"Nothing to be sorry about. He wasn't my father. But, anyway, Maria and Jorge were always with us. We rode our bikes to the park, and while Jorge played basketball at the courts, Maria and I would sit on the sidelines and flirt with all of Jorge's friends. It was nice. At the time, we all thought we were so grown up. We all thought we were moving so fast, but I look at Leila, and all I can think is that at 16, I wouldn't be able to do half of what she had been doing before she was killed. At that age, part of me still thought there was a chance Santa was real."

"Really?" Eric said as Elaine slightly blushed. "Nice childhood."

"I guess," Elaine said, smiling. "And you don't remember where you were?"

"Not really, but if I think hard enough, I was probably getting stoned and listening to Nirvana."

Elaine laughed. She forgot from time to time that Eric was a few years older than her. While he was listening to grunge, she was still playing with dolls.

Eric went on, "I remember wearing baggy jeans and over-sized t-shirts, but speaking of parks, I would go down to one with my best friend Billy, and he would pull a couple of joints out of his pocket, and we would get stoned. Just enough to enjoy the afternoon and be normal before we had to go home for dinner. The park was behind our high school, and we would watch the track team do warm-ups and long distance exercises during practice, and I would think how stupid they were for putting all that effort into running in a circle.

"About a year later, while I was still doing the same 'waste-of-time' activities of my own, Billy and I got caught smoking in the park. I remember the rage on my father's face when he came to the police station. My mother was crying, she thought I was an addict. My father was yelling at the cop, telling him that he was going to take me home and rip down my posters and throw away my CD's. I just sat there blocking everything out. But the one thing I did notice was how cool and calm the cop was. He probably had to put up with enraged people all day long. But he sat there and nodded. He seemed to be so serene because he had the comfort of knowing that he was simply doing his job, he was helping someone's kid. He probably had kids of his own and worried about them every day. And he was doing his job well. He had the power. He had the power to protect and the power to stop bad guys in their tracks. I thought to myself how lucky I was that I wasn't 18 yet because then I would have gone to jail.

"When my parents were driving me home and yelling at me the entire way, I just thought about that cop and how he could have ruined my life, but instead he let my parents work it out with me. It was in that moment that I decided I wanted to be a detective. I wanted to figure out what happened to others so that I could give their families some peace. I never smoked another joint again. And then I joined the track team. I figured I would need the running skills to get through the academy."

"You're a good cop, and you're a good father," Elaine said, patting Eric on the arm.

The two arrived at the restaurant. "Well then, Detective," Elaine said with a wry smile. "We're here. Now what?"

"Well, according to the owner's statement, Leila would have come in after closing, which was midnight. He said that it took anywhere from five to six hours to clean the restaurant, but on this particular day, when he came in at 8:00 a.m. to start cooking, she was still here. The closing manager said she was on time at midnight. Why did it take her so long to clean?"

"No security cameras, right?"

"No. Not one."

"Well, let's think. Are there any 24-hour stores around here? Maybe she ran out to get something," Elaine said, beginning to brainstorm.

"Possible, but that wouldn't add two to three hours onto her work day. She had to have gone somewhere."

"Let's see what we can find," Elaine said as she walked towards the shopping center adjacent to the restaurant. "These places will have security cameras." Eric began to follow her into the shopping center.

"They do, but not all of them would have been open during the middle of the night," Eric called out as he walking briskly after her.

"True, but that doesn't mean the cameras didn't catch something." Eric stopped for a moment, clearly impressed.

The first stop was a small 24-hour convenience store.

As Elaine walked through the front door she saw the man behind the counter and showed him her badge. "Excuse me, but do you have security cameras here?"

A bit astonished, the cashier's eyes got wide. "I don't want any trouble, ma'am. My dad owns the store, I just run it."

"No one's in trouble, sir," Elaine reassured. "My partner and I are doing some investigation on a case we are working on and thought maybe your camera may help us identify someone."

"Well, okay," the cashier said, "what time would they have been in the store?"

Eric spoke up, "Anytime between midnight and 8 a.m."

"That's a long time, but okay. What day?"

"Last Thursday."

"Come with me." The cashier then yelled to someone in the back, in his native language, and an older woman appeared. They exchanged a few words, and she took over the counter.

The cashier escorted Eric and Elaine into the back where his computer sat on his desk. He brought up the security camera feed. On a separate monitor, the detectives could see a screen split into six with cameras all over the store. The cashier typed in the date and time on his computer screen and the frozen images of last Thursday at midnight popped up on the screen.

"This is the button you press to start the images moving. They will all move at the same time. If you want, click the arrow on the double play button here, and you can put everything in fast motion. It's a pretty quiet neighborhood and not too many people come in over night, so I suggest watching it in fast motion to see if anyone pops up." The cashier then got up from his desk and asked the detectives to sit down.

"If you don't mind, I'll stay here in case you have any questions," the cashier said.

"That would be fine. As a matter of fact, have you seen this woman before?" Eric then showed the cashier a picture of Leila.

"Oh yeah, I have seen her in here a lot. I couldn't forget her.

Not only is she really pretty, but her wig was obvious. My mother always pushed me to ask her out because she is clearly Middle Eastern, but to me she always looked too young."

Elaine perked up. "So, then, you did see her here a lot?"

"Oh yes, but she always seemed so alone. Like she was depressed or something. Not too attractive, but she was pretty though." The cashier let out a nervous chuckle and then retreated into his own thoughts.

Eric and Elaine fast-forwarded through the footage, but Leila in her wig was never there on that night. The two detectives thanked the cashier and moved on.

Neither the grocery store, the liquor store, nor the shoe store could provide additional information. These stores either closed between 10 and midnight or their security cameras were not working. When they showed Leila's photo, no one recognized her.

Feeling a little dejected and feeling as if precious time was being wasted, the detectives hit one of the last stores, a pet store.

When Elaine and Eric entered, they did their usual showing of the badges and asking to see the cameras. When they were escorted into the back room and shown the cameras, Eric became a bit more optimistic.

"Why is this one camera turned around towards the store?"

"It's so that we can do a little marketing research and a little surveillance," the shop manager said. "We put our puppies and kittens in the front window display. We check the cameras to see what kind of people will stop and be potential buyers. We market ourselves according to that demography."

"Smart," Elaine said.

Eric's mind turned to his Missy and her constant nagging for a puppy. Eric would laugh at her and said they will be bringing home a new baby instead. Eric imagined Leila standing in front of that window looking at the cute animals. What 16 year old doesn't want a kitten? What kind of 16 year old has her life ripped from her by some madman?

The shop owner, unaware of Eric being lost in his thoughts continued, "Yeah, that's why if you follow any of our social media accounts it's usually directed at young girls and their moms. Dads are always less hesitant to buy a pet. The camera also lets us keep the animals safe in case anyone tries to break the glass or something. Anyway, here is the footage from midnight to 8 a.m. I am not sure if any of it could be of any help, but here you go."

"Thanks," Eric said. The manager went back to watch the floor, and Eric and Elaine fixated on the screen. About 15 minutes later, something caught Eric's eye. "Wait, wait, wait. Go back."

"To where?" Elaine asked.

"Back to 02:47:40. Or somewhere around there."

Elaine backed up the footage.

"Look, look, look, there. Right there!" Eric partially shouted, his eyes wide. Elaine looked intently and after a few moments she realized what Eric saw. The image of a man reflected in the glass of the pet store. A man who looked to be about Leila's age and ethnicity.

"It's kind of blurry. Is there a way to print this out?" Eric bolted back into the store and asked the shop manager to print out the image for them.

"Thank you," Eric said as the two left the store.

"Do you think this means anything?" Elaine asked Eric as they walked back towards the Chinese restaurant.

"Well, let's think. Maybe this guy was on his way to meet Leila at the restaurant."

"Okay."

"Maybe he took her somewhere to do something."

"Or maybe they sat and talked. Wait! Wait a minute. Come with me!" Elaine called out as she ran back towards the pet store. Within the hour, Elaine and Eric had five more print outs of the same man walking past the pet store on various nights, but always during the hours that Leila was working. After spending another hour going back to each store and looking at the angles of their security cameras, they were able to pull two images from the grocery store's camera that not only showed the same man walking across the parking lot from a distance, but this particular camera was in color.

Eric and Elaine got in their car and retraced the rest of Leila's steps, which were as normal as any could be. If she started out at 8 a.m. from the restaurant, the pharmacy opened at nine, and the grocery store at seven, she could have been back home no later than 9:30 or 10. It was apparent from Eric's initial search at 23 Hope Street that Leila did her laundry in the house.

Out of fresh ideas, the detectives returned to the station.

Elaine knocked on Eric's door and said, "Our guys were able to enhance the images and clear them up a bit. This seems to be the guy that may have visited Leila." Elaine put all the photos down on the desk. The colorful images provided the best visualization.

Eric thought out loud, "So, here's a guy who visits Leila at work on several occasions. What do they talk about? What does he convince her to do?"

"Perhaps he convinces her to meet him in the park?"

"Perhaps, but can it be that easy?"

"Whatever they talk about, it takes a lot of planning on his part because it took several attempts at visiting her."

"Why visit her at work and not at home?"

"Maybe because of Louisa?"

"Maybe, but still. Why hide?"

With that Elaine's eyes got wide. Eric looked at her and could see something was brewing inside of her mind. A second later she looked up at Eric, "Look. Look at what he is wearing."

Eric could not see anything that was that distinguishing in the photo. "What?"

Elaine pointed to the man's pants, "Green. His pants are green."

"So?"

"So, the guy who Louisa saw in the park. The Green Ghost."

"Wait, what?"

"The Green Ghost. If this guy is always sneaking around, if

maybe Leila told Louisa she was imagining things or..."

"...Or trying to get her not to talk or..."

"Or showing her a photo of someone and saying the person was dead, but then you see him in a park..."

"He would be a..."

"Ghost," the two detectives said in unison.

After some silence Eric said, "I think whoever this guy is, he killed Leila to get to Louisa."

CHAPTER 23

Our Facebook page was filling up. Not only did we post there, but our followers did, too.

"Our page is open to anyone who wants to participate, comment, add, share, or suggest" was written on the top of the page.

I defined myself as the moderator of the page and every now and then when I thought that a post might offend or hurt someone's feelings, I didn't hesitate to delete it.

Once a week, on Sundays, I took it upon myself to post an exercise that would spark and challenge our followers' minds. On some occasions, there were mathematical riddles with a hundred ways to solve them. Sometimes my posts were riddles or puns, and sometimes they were short stories or ideas that crossed my mind in the middle of the night.

People wrote, responded, and added ideas of their own.

They posted ideas taken from different cultures, which encouraged them to see the world in a different way. On our side, we willingly shared the stage with everyone.

A follower, named Cynthia, posted the following: "First I put the pie into the oven, then I have time to sit down and think about the ingredients."

Nick, one of my students, posted the following riddle: "You're walking down the street. Accidentally you step on a pile of sand. It looks like golden sand from the beach, but it's not. As soon as you step on the pile, the sand becomes quicksand and locks your feet in. Now you're stuck. You cannot move. Luckily for you, you're holding a laptop. What would you do? How would you release yourself from the sand?"

"LOL," a follower named Tom commented. "I'll be searching Google for how to free myself from quicksand."

Another follower named Justin5 wrote: "I have a riddle for you. Read the following story and try to answer the question at the end.

"Roberto turned 50 years old. His wife surprised him and fulfilled an old dream: an invitation to a skydiving session accompanied by an instructor. When the man returned home, he felt great. 'I did it,' he whispered to himself.

"He opened up his desk drawer and took out a brown notebook. On the first page was his bucket list: 35 dreams to fulfill before death. Roberto took a pen and crossed out the first thing on the list—skydiving. He decided that by the end of that day he must complete the second dream on his list.

"Please note that Roberto has less than 8 hours to accomplish the second task, and no, there's no connection between the first mission and the second. In fact, his second task is not related to extreme sports .

"Your task: Try to guess what the second thing on his bucket list is.

"Yes, every guess may work, there's no right or wrong answer, but try to get inside the head of our hero Roberto, who just turned 50 today and returned back home alive after jumping from an airplane. (Hint: Think what you would do if you were in that situation.)"

I logged out of our Facebook page. I was proud. Our followers not only liked our page but also added their own creative ideas. I was satisfied like a cat that found the milk jug. Does it mean we are really working toward our goal? Does it mean that people really appreciate our tools and are working with us to become open minded? It took me a second to log in to our Facebook page again. I started typing fast before I forgot: "Make up your own stories."

EXERCISE NO. 8

For the next exercise we have gathered a list of places around the world. This is not just another list. These are real places, cities, and towns that no one knows the story behind their odd name. Show your creativity. Make up any story that answers the question: why was this place named in such a way?

Remember, there's no good nor bad story. Everything is subject to your interpretation.

Names of unconventional streets, cities, and towns:

1. "Hell"—a large city located in the state of Michigan.
2. "No Name"—This is not a typo. That's the official name of the river, a tunnel, and a shopping mall. All three are located within the state of Colorado"No Name Creek and No Name Canyon."
3. "Chicken"—the name of a city in Alaska. (Is that where the first chicken was found and what came first, the "chicken" or the egg?)
4. "Monster" —In the Netherlands there's a nice village named Monster. Its people are very friendly.
5. "Why"—No, it's not a question from our previous exercise. In Arizona there is a town called "Why." Could someone explain to me why?
6. "Hungry Horse"—There are probably some hungry horses in the State of Montana.
7. "Nothing" —That's the name of a small town in Arizona. I wonder what the address on the envelope looks like?
8. "Lost" —a small village in Scotland. Did anyone get lost

there once?

9. "Monkey's Eyebrow"—a rural community in Kentucky. I just hope that the mayor keeps his eyebrows neat.

∽⌘∾

"My Group B was really crazy about this exercise," wrote Drew in our group chat. It was a great opening for our first spring session. Each student added another piece to the story. I'm proud to present our class story about a town named Hell."

"Do you know why it was decided to call a town in Michigan "Hell"? No, it's not a coincidence. One day, in 1898, a casual visitor came to town. Actually he was just on his way to Cleveland, Ohio, but his horse was tired, and he decided to give his aching back a little rest. It was a cold December day, and the snow covered the path. He was holding a small lamp to illuminate his way. It was close to midnight when he finally crossed the path to a ghost town. A big creaky iron sign was half hanging on the tree. The sign read: "Welcome to Hell."

From a distance, he saw a faint light coming from one of the houses. Hoping that the coins in his pocket would get him a nice bed and a hot meal for one day, he got off the horse and knocked on the door. No one answered. He knocked again and heard footsteps approaching. The heavy wooden door creaked open, and an elderly man looked at him. "What do you want?" he barked.

"Excuse me, sir. I'm really sorry for bothering you. Maybe you could let me sleep here tonight? I'm tired and hungry, and my horse needs some rest. I have some coins that I can give you in return."

"Go to hell," the old man slammed the door angrily.

Our man was sad but refused to give up. He led his horse through the trails that were covered with ice and headed to another house. Gently he knocked. An old lady opened the door and once again she slammed the door at his face and cursed, "Go to hell." The same thing repeated itself at the third and fourth house.

Our guy was sad and exhausted, and without any other options, he pulled an old wool blanket from his saddle pack and spread it beneath the iron gate that greeted him "to Hell." With his horse by his side, he fell asleep.

He woke up at dawn. Lit a small fire to warm his bones. Then, washed his face in the icy water puddles. He was trembling. "I'm not staying in this town," he muttered to himself. "I'm sorry." He stroked the back of the horse. "I know you're tired, but we must go on." He climbed on its back.

His eyes darkened, and his hair froze. On the top of the hill, not far from the heavy iron gate was a cheery-looking hostel. The name of the lodge was: "Go to Hell."

Our Facebook page was flooded with responses too. "Have you heard about a town called 'Accident' in Maryland?" Sara asked. "I believe that it was named after a famous math problem: Two trains leave different cities heading toward each other at different speeds. When and where do they meet?"

What about "Try Again? The name of a town in South Africa," Tunica wrote on our page. What do you think the story is here? I have a feeling that there was once a businessman who succeeded in nothing, or a desperate mother who decided to buy her son a village?

"Pee Town in Ohio," Sabrina pointed out, "I believe they have the best urinal in the world!"

CHAPTER 24

The motive question drove Eric crazy. Once again he dug into the data that was pinned on sticky notes to the corkboard in his office.

There were many questions but no answers.

Why was Leila murdered?

Why did Leila use a fake passport to enter the country?

Why is there no record of Louisa entering the States?

Why did they decide to settle in Providence, Rhode Island?

Why did they have to hide their identities and use synthetic wigs?

Why was this guy in the park following Louisa?

Why was there another stick figure in Leila's drawing?

Why wasn't the name Hamdi mentioned before?

Why did Leila change her routine the day of the murder?

Why did she invite the babysitter to come earlier that day?

Why didn't she tell anybody where she was going or when she would return?

Why is this investigation getting so complicated?

The phone buzzed on his desk. "Yes?" he snapped.

"Eric, there's a private call for you. It's your mother-in-law," said George and connected the line.

"Hello?"

"Eric? I'm sorry for calling the station. We tried your cell phone, but there was no answer."

He pulled out his cell phone from his pocket and cursed quietly. The battery was dead.

"Yes, Margaret. What's going on? Is everything okay with Dina?"

"Dina...she tried to call you...she's on her way to the hospital."

Eric jumped from his chair. "Shit," he cursed. "Has it started?" Work was suddenly forgotten, and Eric could feel his heart pounding. Dina was due in three weeks or so and hadn't even reached her 37th week.

"Yes, the taxi took her to the hospital a few minutes ago. I was here helping her do laundry when, all of a sudden, she had a sharp pain and her water broke. You need to go to the hospital, Eric, she needs you."

Eric glanced at the clock. It was nearly 3:00 p.m. "What about Missy?"

"Don't worry. I'll pick her up from pre-school, and she can stay as long as need be. You go off to the hospital."

"Thank you, Margaret." He breathed deeply as he grabbed his coat and headed for the door.

Why? Eric thought as he ran across the parking lot toward his car. *Why must life always get so complicated?*

At the hospital Eric learned that the delivery was also complicated. The baby was breech.

"We need to perform a C-section because the delivery started after the water broke and any further delay could endanger the baby," the doctor said.

Dina said nothing, but Eric could tell she was scared. He held her hand tightly and kissed her forehead.

"Okay," Eric nodded, trying to give Dina a look of reassurance, which he felt was short of the mark.

"Right," the doctor said calmly and efficiently. "I'll go get ready. And try not to worry too much; at 36 weeks the baby is going to be just fine."

It was 4:15 p.m. when Eric accompanied Dina's bed to the operating room, but they didn't allow him beyond the door. He hugged Dina and whispered, "Everything will be fine, my love. I promise. I'll be here waiting for you." He kissed her softly on the lips. "Just think that pretty soon," he choked on the words, "soon...we will have a sweet baby to hold. A sibling for our Missy."

Later on, even as he was doing it, Eric realized he'd turned into the stereotypical pacing expectant father as he walked back and forth across the waiting room. The clock on the wall showed that it was almost 6:00, and no doctor came with either good news or bad, but Eric knew that no news was good news.

He was stressed and in spite of having two cups of coffee, felt no guilt when he placed the third on the table next to the well-worn sofa. Worn, Eric surmised, by years of expectant fathers and families flopping in and popping off the furniture. The waiting, the doing nothing, drove him just short of crazy.

He recalled the words that the doctor whispered before they rolled Dina's bed to the surgery room, "Everything should be okay, but we have to get her into surgery now. I'm sorry, but it might take longer than usual."

Eric's hand had been shaking when he signed the consent form. He decided not to worry Dina with the small print. "Just bring them back both safe," he'd pleaded with the doctor.

Eric also couldn't help but think of Leila. He wondered if she was as shaky then and he is now when she had to make the choice to bring Louisa to America by illegal means. He began to wonder what could have possibly been going through her head while she was dying. Would her baby be taken care of? Would she be safe? Was there anyone else in this world that was capable of caring for Louisa better than her own mother?

He walked around in the waiting room and stopped to look outside the window. The beautiful colors of the sky at sunset calmed him down. As the light faded, only a few people were crossing the streets, and cars were racing home from work.

God, he prayed silently, *I know I don't pray often enough but please, let them both get through this safely.* The big wall clock ticked again. It was 6:30 now. He scratched his forehead. *Oh God, how much longer?*

Eric had already made some calls from the pay phone in the hallway because hospitals don't appreciate cell phones and besides, his phone was dead. He'd called his parents, Dina's parents, and his sister, but there wasn't much he could tell them.

Missy, he learned, was doing fine. She'd spent the afternoon playing with her dolls and was told that her parents would be home soon. In the meantime her Papa and Nana had made her favorite food: pasta with meatballs.

He checked his cell phone for the fifth time and, although he already knew, he still felt annoyed when he saw that the battery was dead. This was despite the fact that he couldn't use it anyway within the confines of the hospital. Everything, it seemed, was conspiring to make him feel more isolated and, if he was honest, absolutely powerless.

As a parent, he did not like that feeling. He didn't like not being able to care for his child. Although he didn't want to entertain the thought, he wondered what kind of parent he would be if anything was to happen to Dina. Could he raise Missy on his own? Could he raise two children on his own?

He needed to distract his mind so he asked one of the nurses if they had a charger for his old model. He didn't quite appreciate the joke when an orderly laughed and said, "Try the Fossil

Museum." Dina had been right when, a few months ago, she'd suggested he get an upgrade. She was always right.

He sipped the cold coffee and it tasted exactly like coffee from a vending machine always does: metallic. On the first floor, they served better coffee, but he was afraid to leave his spot in the waiting room. What if the doctor came looking for him?

Instead, he continued to pace, aware that he not only looked like a lion in a cage but that he also felt like one. The waiting was driving him insane.

Another family entered the waiting area. A three-year-old girl was among the group. Eric figured it was the father, the grandparents, and the granddaughter. She reminded him of Missy and how she too was waiting for her new younger sibling to come home. His mind began to drift again, and he thought about Louisa.

As the thoughts of Louisa come into his mind, another man came in but gave Eric no more than a cursory nod before sitting down on the worn couch. Another anxious body wearing away the fabric, Eric thought. It was only seconds before the man's eyelids began to flicker as sleep overcame him. Eric kept glancing over to the man and wondered just how he could appear so unconcerned. This wasn't, and could never be in Eric's mind, the right time to take a nap.

He'd been worried enough when Missy was born and that pregnancy and labor had been relatively trouble free. This time the scales fell heavily on the side of worry, and it was hard to feel excited. If it all went well then, any moment now, the doctor would come out and tell him that everything was fine with both of them. Yet, all he would feel this time around was relief.

On the other hand, if anything went wrong, Eric knew, perhaps better than most people that life can change in an instant. That the world may tip over in seconds. He recalled the weeping families who were in his office over the years. Death by stabbing takes a few seconds. Cardiac arrest can take even less than that.

Stabbing. Leila. Louisa. Louisa will never know what it is to be an older sibling. Her mother will never be alive again to have another baby. Of course, her father can have more children, but where is that father? Is he alive? Why is he not with Louisa? Did Leila run away from him? Why is he a mystery within this mystery?

He turned and took a long look at the man on the sofa. He was definitely sleeping now, his breathing deep and heavy. Eric felt a mixture of annoyance and shock surge through him. How could the man not be anxious? Not seem, at least on the surface, to be even a little concerned?

A man in such situations, waiting for the doctor's verdict, can get positively excited and wait anxiously, or be very concerned and pray that everything goes well. But apathy? There is no such option. Having a baby is the most wonderful thing in the world, isn't it? And the man had shown no emotion toward anyone, not even Eric, who was, after all, an obviously anxious father to be. Why would a man not apparently care about the outcome? Why...? Unless....

Suddenly his mind switched back to cop mode. *Unless, of course, you don't want the baby for whatever reason.* Maybe it would just be another mouth to feed or, perhaps, be an embarrassment? Maybe you wouldn't want your wife to find out, or someone else.

Maybe it would be better for all concerned if the baby, and perhaps the mother too, never existed, ceased to exist, and could never tell your secret either now or in the future? Pride, he already knew, could be an extremely strong motivator when it came to murder.

"Jesus Christ!" he exclaimed out loud, startling the sleeping man who jolted upright and glared at him still without saying a word.

"Aha! Now I get it! Now everything makes sense!" Eric shouted at the stunned father-to-be as he rushed from the room and headed straight for the payphone.

"The Green Ghost is the father," he said, as soon as Elaine picked up.

"What? Why? Eric...where are you?"

He ignored her final question. "For whatever reason, he was hiding his own indiscretion," he shouted into the phone. "Whatever happened between him and Leila, he didn't want it revealed. All he has been doing is simply eliminating the evidence, and the other piece of evidence is likely to be Louisa."

"Sorry, Eric, but you're going a little too fast for me, and," she repeated, "where are you anyway?"

"I'll tell you later, but listen, Elaine, alert the officers who are patrolling the foster parent's house. There's a good chance that he will try and kill the girl. Whatever drove him to kill Leila means it's likely the job isn't finished yet. Get on to it straight away, will you?"

At that precise moment the door opened and the doctor came out into the waiting room with a smile on his face.

CHAPTER 25

From the darkest mind of a potential killer:

People walk in circles. Chasing their shadows.
No need to think. Just go. Place their feet in the
footprints that were left in the sand by their
predecessors. Heel by heel. One foot after the
other.

Where would they go? They stare at the bare
back of their brothers. Their necks are covered
with ropes. The groom is not. Today is the day
of the feast.

Their voices make unclear sounds. Tunes they
inherited from their previous generations.
"Aaaah .... Tzm. Tzmaha" is repeated as the
melody rises above the wind of the African

deserts.

Through it all the drums are heard. Fists pounding the drums. Boom and whack... is all you hear. Leaping legs, beating the hard ground. Burning sand. Stones underfoot. Who cares? You must be happy. You must thank the gods.

It's just a ritual. Abstract symbols. It is not reality. Not what it appears to be.

The men wake up at dawn to get ready for the ceremony. Wash in cold water left in their honor by their women. They are the first to start the fire. A big fire that would not extinguish before the sky is lit with stars.

The groom needs to be prepared, to smear his body with that muddy mixture of sheep body fat and droppings. It smells disgusting, but the groom is happy. The horrible smell takes away the evil eye of the gods living in the underworld, giving him hope for a long life.

When everything is ready, they kneel and sacrifice the first camel to the gods and offer the head to the gods.

Now it is time to dance in front of the fire. The dancing stops when they bring the bride over from the women's tent.

Everyone dance together. It's a feast for the whole family and the whole tribe. If the gods do not feel the inner joy, they may punish you. The drums beat faster. You must dance faster. Stomping the feet. The women are getting closer. You can hear their loud cries of joy coming up from their throats, welcoming the bride. The older women of the tribe are escorting the bride. Thrashing lightly the bride with sticks. It is a good sign. This keeps the misfortune away. Wishing the bride success in bearing many sons. The women circle the fire twice. Then the ceremony begins.

They fall down onto the ground, kissing it while crying. This is their crying prayer to the gods. They weep, cry, and beg for mercy and for good fortune, all in honor of the couple getting married today. The louder they cry, the better the chance that the gods may hear them and bless the couple.

Then, it is over.

And now they are ready. The women get up and move away from the fire. The men can return. The women retire to their tent. They will be back shortly to bring food for the men and serve them. Women are forbidden to taste this food or to make eye contact with the men whom they serve. They will display the food before them and leave. Once they are gone, the men may enjoy their meal.

Evening comes. The loud sound of drums continues. Feet are jumping and dancing. Tired throats must sing. Now the women are allowed to return. This time the bride's face will be covered by a veil. The groom removes the veil and examines her to see if he's satisfied.

Yes, he smiles. Now it's his turn to sing the song. "I accept this burden," he sings.

The groom covers the bride's face and neck with a small scarf interwoven with copper coins. It must encompass the entire face and neck. No bare skin should be seen.

It is over. They are married. They must continue to dance and sing until the fire goes out. The ceremony is done. From here everyone goes back to their tents.

The bride and groom will now enter their wedding tent.

Blessed are the gods.

Today was my wedding day.

CHAPTER 26

My second YouTube movie clip gained much interest. I posted the link on our Facebook page and found out later that it was hash-tagged in other social media platforms. I was happy and excited about our popularity. "It's real!" I exclaimed in our group chat. "People like it, they find interest in our idea, and they follow us!"

"What do I do now?" I went back to ask my social media expert, my student Johnny, who came up with the YouTube clip idea in the first place.

"I don't know," he replied, "make another video clip?"

"Okay, and then what? Do I just keep recording videos? Is there any other way to spread the word?"

"I don't know," he shrugged. "Maybe write a huge sign across the sky." He laughed. "Well, come on, be creative! You are the one who told us there are no boundaries to thinking. Come up with a breakthrough idea!" He laughed again.

"Thanks, Johnny." I returned his grin.

"No matter what you do," he said, "just keep them coming. Keep bringing those exercises."

I clicked the camera button on my computer and clip number 3 was on its way to the YouTube crowd.

Exercise No. 9

Marketing association

The following exercise is a popular one in business schools. The purpose of the exercise is to come up with an idea for an advertisement, linking two things that are not related.

This exercise relates to our second principle, make connections.

Read the following situation and come up with your own ideas:

You work at a marketing and public relations department in a private company. One day an important customer comes into your office and wants to hire you to promote his new business. Please note—our client is about to launch his brilliant idea! A nationwide network of stores for Build-It-Yourself refrigerators. The stores are designed for customers who are interested in buying a new refrigerator, but why should they settle for what the manufacturer chose for them, if they can choose themselves?

Yes, at this store you can choose the size, height, color, door designs, and even the compressor size. Not sure what to pick? Try this mix and match. Would you like a refrigerator with three or more doors? You got it! How about transparent doors so you can see what's inside without opening the doors? Lights of different colors? Different kinds of levers? Two drawers or five drawers? You got your wish!

You like the idea? Excellent! Now let's learn how to market it.

But just before the customer leaves the office, he throws the last bombshell into the room. "By the way," he says, "my wife really loves shoes. Before I left the house this morning she requested to see pictures of shoes in this advertisement. It doesn't matter what kind of shoes. The main thing is to have a big picture. There's no problem with that, right?" he calls over his shoulder before disappearing.

Remember—a picture is a worth thousand words. Adding a picture is important and it must be integrated into your advertisement. The power of the photo is in representing the first impression. With the right image you can gain attention.

Most companies are looking for a picture that represents, in a logical way, their product. For example, car companies use racing horses to display speed. Baby food companies will use smiling babies or kids in their advertisements, etc.

What we ask you to do is the opposite. We ask you to attract your customer's attention with the no logical connection.

Back to our situation. Take a deep breath. You are in the marketing business. You must find the link between shoes and refrigerators. What do you do?

Before we give you time to make up the connection, here is our technique:

First select a picture of shoes. Yes, start with a big picture. Now take a blank sheet of paper. Tape the picture of shoes at the top of the page. Under that, make a list of descriptive words that come to mind when you think of shoes. (Remember—words that evoke emotion are important.)

Here's a list of our examples: shoes are strong, beautiful, comfortable, modern, colorful, multicolor, different styles, match other clothing or a belt, can be found in varying sizes, they make walking comfortable, they have laces, thick soles, leather, plastic or cloth, slippers, high heels, and so on.

Now take another page and write down all the attributes and associations that come to mind when you see a refrigerator. For example:

White, silver, or black, big, strong, bulky, making noise, cold, tidy shelves, sturdy, things get lost, keeping food fresh, and so on.

Here's an important tip: any online search engine will help you find more adjectives for shoes and refrigerators. Just look up words and phrases (including slang) and your worldview is enriched in an instant.

Now let's try to connect them.

How about...

"Are your steel shoes more comfortable than your refrigerator? It's time to move on to the advanced refrigerator."

Here's another one:

"The shoes you chose are from the designer shop, but not the refrigerator? Choose the design that fits your size!"

It is also possible to use slang phrases: "Don't be a shoe, switch today to the most advanced refrigerator."

Last but not least: "Have you heard about grandma's shoes? Good, leave it for your grandma. For yourself, get the most advanced refrigerator in the world."

Now it's your turn to practice.

Let's go back to the same situation. You work in a marketing job. Your client is ready to spend money to promote and market his business. But there's one condition. He wants to choose the image that will be used.

Pay attention to the following details:

The business: car dealership—replace an old car with a newer model (with no downpayment).

The image that was chosen for you: A set of colorful balloons (like his child always wanted).

Your task is to find advertising ideas that are connecting cars and balloons.

Ready? Go!

CHAPTER 27

It was almost nine p.m. when Eric entered Missy's room. "My princess," he whispered in her ear, "it's time to go to bed." Missy snuggled deep into her father's arms. "My daddy is a hero," she whispered while resting her head on his shoulder.

Eric's heart melted.

It had been three days since returning home with the new baby girl, and Eric promised himself he'd put his family first. He knew that at times his job meant being needed at unexpected hours, but he'd promised himself, and Dina, that on regular days he'd be back home no later than 6:30.

They'd named the baby Angel, because in her parents' eyes she was a perfect creation. Eric couldn't help but think about Louisa, and he couldn't shake off the possibility that her father was actually out to kill her.

Eric said nothing, but kissed his daughter's hair and covered her with a blanket. Then, he bent down on his knees next to her bed and kissed her on the cheeks and nose. Missy giggled.

"Daddy?"

"Yes, sweetheart?"

"Daddy, why do we have these little flashing lights on our windows and doors in the house?"

"Those are sensors," he explained. "They protect us from bad people."

"Why are there bad people?"

"Because," he thought for a moment, "because sometimes good people do bad things."

"So bad people can be good people but they just do bad things?"

"Umm...yes, I guess that's true. Sometimes they want to do bad things, sometimes they have to do bad things, and sometimes they are just plain stupid."

Missy took the time to think about it. "You know what?" she asked. "It's like the story Miss Lynn told us this morning about the giant man that every time kids wanted to play in his magic garden he would stand next to the window and call: 'No kids, no play! Kids go away!' All the children were scared, but then everyone understood that he's not a bad man, he just didn't want kids to fall down and break their heads. It's the same thing, right? So bad people can actually be good, right?"

"I guess so...yeah...something like that."

His cell phone rang interrupting the conversation.

"Eric Gutenheim," he said, seeing the call was from the station.

"Eric, it's George. We have a bit of a situation here."

"What's the matter?" Eric asked with concern.

"It's not the end of the world, but one of the men patrolling the foster parents' home has some kind of family emergency. He needs to go home for an hour and we can't find anyone else to cover in the meantime. Is it all right if we leave the house with just one patrol officer until the other returns?"

Eric thought long and hard about this. Would it really be the end of the world if for one night the Johnsons had a peaceful, normal evening, with just one patrolling officer instead of two? As Eric was about to utter the word "Okay," he looked at the blinking security lights on the windows and his Missy falling fast asleep.

"You know what, George, I don't feel comfortable with that. Does this guy need the entire night off?"

"No, it's just for one hour, Eric, but he's already left to go help his family."

"I'm on my way, George. I'll cover the shift in the meantime, and we'll have the other officer cover me just in case."

Eric got to the Johnsons' house just before 9:30 p.m. He thought to himself that it would only be one hour, maybe one and a half, not more. Dina wasn't too happy about it, but she understood. She texted her mom and put her on call in case she needed any help with the baby, but fortunately, Angel was sleeping well.

First, Eric made sure to greet the other patrol officer on site, then he did a quick walk around the house to make sure everything looked normal, and he checked in with the Johnsons via cell phone as to not disturb Louisa. Eric didn't want Louisa to know that someone was guarding the house. He wanted her experience to feel as normal as possible. Mrs. Johnson was nice enough to put some coffee in a thermos for the patrol officers so that they could stay alert until the end of their shift. She also prepared some small snack sandwiches for both officers, for which they were extremely grateful.

Eric couldn't help but feel nostalgic as he sat in his car about 20 yards away from the Johnson's home. This scenario took him back to his early days as a detective. He would do frequent stakeouts like this one. He even had one stakeout where he had to disguise himself as a server in an ice cream parlor in order to keep tabs on an organized crime boss. All these years and several promotions later, he was going back to basics.

To keep himself occupied, Eric went through the facts. He began to mismatch them one against the other in the hope that something would jump out at him.

It seemed pretty straightforward: a mother and child are escaping their country to come to America to live a new life. A classic story. But why the wigs?

A young mother is murdered; does she know her killer? In this situation it seemed likely. Is the killer associated with Louisa? Does Louisa know this person? Is this person the third person in the child's picture?

The facts and theories just kept coming at him. After about 45 minutes, Eric couldn't stay in one place, so he decided to take a walk.

Eric got out of the car and started walking towards the Johnsons' house. The breeze was a bit cool, but the air was not cold. It almost refreshed Eric's mind. The wind began to kick up some with sharp gusts that almost knocked Eric off balance.

There must be a storm coming.

Eric thought that he would do another walk around the premises.

The theories and disconnected parts kept coming. A child in a wig/a Chinese restaurant, the Muslim/the Coptic Christians of Egypt/a walk in the park, a stalker/a landlord with something to hide, a guy in green shorts/a murder by stabbing, a tidy murder scene/a pendant with symbols, all of these facts kept flipping through his mind. It reminded him of the card game the girls were playing with Louisa in the hospital. One word leads to another.

All seemed clear around the Johnsons' house. Eric kept walking around the house anyway, thinking. Muslim: this was a religion he should know more about, but as his trip to Father John proved, there is a large Christian Coptic population in the Middle Eastern world as well as Muslims, so that meant Leila must have been from the Arab world, which can be Christian or Muslims, yet, either way she was likely from the Arabian Peninsula .

Her supposed sect of Bedouin Tribe, Al-Miiarkh, was from

the Kalahari, so that meant central-southern Africa, and the Koran found in her apartment, doubtfully hers, meant Muslim.

Yet, the Koran was dusty, which also indicated that she was not very religious or was non-Muslim. The investigation into the restaurant found that there were African dishwashers who practiced Islam, but they didn't really speak to Leila. They did, however, clear up that a dusty Koran would not be found in the home of a devout Muslim.

What makes someone break away from his religion? Eric hadn't practiced Catholicism in a long time, but that was common of many Catholics. But, Eric also knew that a rift in beliefs causes a person to leave his religion or take a step back from it.

Did Leila not agree with Muslim tradition? Or if she was a Christian, how come they didn't find any Christian symbols in her apartment? Was she an atheist? Did she believe is something completely different?

Eric made another turn around the house.

No good. Opposite of good is bad. Did Leila do something bad?

The wind blew again causing the tree branches to squeak. After a week with a new baby, the creaking almost sounded like a baby's whine in the middle of the night.

Baby. Louisa. Was Louisa "the thing" that Leila did wrong?

Marriage. The pendant suggests that Leila was married. If she was married and had a baby, then all was well. Why leave her husband? Did he beat her? Her autopsy didn't come up with any trauma or scarring. The only inconsistency was a small prick on the tip of her finger that was surmised to be some work injury.

Eric made another turn around the house.

Did Louisa have anything to do with this at all? An Arabic interpreter had been brought in to talk to her, but she understood Arabic as much as she understood English, and in either language she didn't remember much about her life.

The picture. What was she trying to say in the picture? Was he the bad man that has been tracking her down her whole life? Tracking her down to kill her like he killed her mother? He killed her mother for some reason. A reason that had to do with the pendant, the killer's mark, to somehow prove what he did was honorable.

Honor.

It was an honor killing, thought Eric. What did Leila do to her husband? She left. She left him without his permission. That is all it could be. Is the Green Ghost her husband?

Eric stopped. He felt he was onto something.

A harsh gust of wind blew up again. Eric braced himself. The wind died down, but the rustling of the leaves in the trees made Eric look up. The moonlight was illuminating one of the windows, and it was clear it was a little girl's room. Eric wondered if the Johnsons had done the room over to make Louisa feel at home. He looked at his watch. It was 10:30. The house was dark, and everyone was asleep. A thought occurred to Eric: is Louisa safe in that room? The thought came into Eric's head as he was standing under the tree, so step by step he began to climb it.

When Eric got up to eye level with the window, the moonlight was shining in the room, and he could see the outline of Louisa's small body in the bed. He inched closer to the edge of the branch in order to see if it was possible to get to the window. As Eric got closer, the branch began to bend under his weight. He moved a little bit further to see exactly at what point he felt the branch might snap. He began to calculate that a person with a much smaller stature than his own could possibly get to the edge, but the branch was far enough away to prevent any entrance into the house. But still, Eric thought, a peeping tom could sit here and watch.

As the thought sent chills through Eric and his stomach turned, he focused on something that was reflecting in the window. It was just above his head and was slowly coming into focus. Eric couldn't figure it out at first, but it seemed as if it might be a squirrel. As Eric blinked hard to adjust his sight in the moonlight, another gust of wind blew up separating the branches and leaves as Eric closed his eyes to prevent dirt and leaves from getting into his eyes, the smaller twig branches began to slap him in the face. As one whipped him in the ear, he thrust open his eyes in pain and in the window staring back at him was the reflection of a man's face just one foot above Eric. Eric widened his eyes, opened his mouth, and as he was about to scream, the body heaved itself down onto Eric, taking both of them out of the tree and onto the ground below.

Eric didn't have time to cry out from the pain that seared through his body as he hit the grass because the man was on top of him with his hands around his throat.

Eric grabbed the man's wrists and tried to pull his hands from around his neck. As Eric did this move, he was able to regain some strength and throw the man off him. It was an easy task as this man was half the size of Eric, but equally as strong.

Eric tried to get to his feet, but the man charged at him knocking him back down again, but Eric was able to grip onto the man's body and thrust him away as Eric fell once again to the ground.

Eric quickly got to his feet, as did the other man who started yelling at Eric in what seemed to be an Arabic language.

The wind gusted, moving the tree branches and allowing moonlight to come through, shedding some light on the man with an olive complexion. The branches moved in another direction causing the moonlight to reflect off of the downstairs window of the house and illuminated the man's outfit; an ill-fitting t-shirt...and green shorts.

The Green Ghost is no ghost.

"STOP," the Green Ghost yelled at Eric.

"Who are you?" Eric yelled back.

"NO!"

As the Green Ghost charged at Eric, there was a gunshot that pierced through the air. The Green Ghost fell to the ground and placed his hands behind his head. Eric looked around and saw the other police officer from the precinct standing on the front lawn with his gun drawn in Eric's direction.

All the lights in the Johnsons' house came on. Eric looked

down at the Green Ghost while putting the handcuffs on him as the other officer said: "You have the right to remain silent. Anything you say can and will be used against you in a court of law. You have the right to an attorney. If you cannot afford an attorney, one will be provided for you. Do you understand the rights I have just read to you?"

“’”

"Eric..."

"What?"

"Try not to tear him apart, okay? You're hellishly close to this, you know, and we're not absolutely certain of anything yet and can't book him for loitering in a tree."

"Loitering in a tree? He tried to kill me."

"He had no idea that you were an officer."

"Let's just do this, Elaine."

"Fine."

Eric gave Elaine a knowing look and followed through with a sharp nod.

They entered interrogation room Number 3 and the Green Ghost was sitting on a wooden chair handcuffed to the chair's back.

"Good evening," said Eric. "My name is Detective Gutenheim and I'm the Chief Officer of the Providence police station. This is Sergeant Elaine Hernandez, the deputy. We need to ask you some questions."

The man didn't respond. He sat quietly, a smug look on his face and seemingly unaffected by events. His face expressed nothing but apathy.

Both Eric and Elaine had already been thrown a little off-guard. This was not what they had been expecting.

The man, or kid, looked to be no more than a teenager himself. Maybe 16 or 17 years old they guessed.

"Do you understand what I'm saying?" Eric asked. "Do you understand English? Do you want an interpreter?"

"Yes, I know English. I'm not stupid. No interpreter. No lawyer. No people in the room!"

Eric cut to the chase. Boy or not, this was a probable and potential murderer in front of him. Besides, gang warfare often meant kids were capable of killing. "What were you doing in that yard?" Eric's question was met with an insolent silence, and the man's eyes remained fixed on the table.

"Okay," Eric continued. "Let's start with the simplest questions. Tell us your first and last name?"

Again silence.

"Stop playing games with us!" said Eric. "We've got your picture on the way to FBI, and we will identify you. We already know who you are." Obviously it was a lie, but Eric had to verify that this guy was the man or boy they were looking for.

Silence.

Eric and Elaine exchanged glances.

"I understand," said Eric. "You don't really want to cooperate with us." His voice was calm, but he felt his pulse begin to accelerate. He didn't like this boy, his arrogance, his clear superiority. This wasn't a cocky street kid, this was someone who truly believed he should not be held accountable for his actions. But he was also the only person who knew what had really happened and if Louisa was still in danger. Eric decided to turn the aggressive notch down a little.

"So, let's start from the end. Why did you kill Leila?"

The man raised his eyes for a second, looked at Eric, and then looked back down to the table.

Eric let out an exaggerated sigh, but it was truly how he felt. He was finding it difficult to control his temper. He gave the boy's chair a sharp kick. "Now you listen very carefully. We can make it easy for you or very difficult." Eric used his left hand to raise the boy's chin so he could look straight into his dark eyes. "Do you understand me now?"

He looked into Eric's eyes but said nothing. The arrogant insolence remained. His look reminded Eric of how an exotic prince or some other high authority might behave if threatened. Like they were beyond that kind of thing. Like they could never be held accountable for anything.

"Okay, one minute, Eric," Elaine pulled out the chair and sat next to the boy. "Listen, we understand this situation is hard for you. We just want to ask you a few questions, and then we will let you go back to your cell to eat something and rest. In the morning you'll meet your defense attorney appointed for you by the court, and he or she will talk to you about the whole process. Okay?"

The boy looked at the detectives and did not respond.

Elaine placed her hand on his shoulder. The boy immediately reacted by shaking his shoulder to push her hand away.

Elaine ignored the rebuff and remained calm. "You want us to bring you something to drink? Maybe some water?"

"Yes," he said.

"Great. Here, you see, we're making some progress." She managed a half-smile and then signaled to the police officer stationed at the door. He left and returned with a cup of water and a straw already inserted to allow the man to drink without attempting to use his cuffed hands.

"You know what?" said Elaine. "If you answer some simple questions I may be able to convince Eric here to remove your handcuffs and then you'd feel better, right?"

The boy didn't reply.

"Okay," Elaine continued to keep a positive tone. "So just tell us your full name, age, and where you live?"

More silence.

"Come on, kid." Elaine tried to encourage him patiently saying, "Give us your full name. I'm sure you know it."

Again silence.

Despite his promise to Elaine, Eric felt his patience drain from him. "What the hell is the matter with you, boy? I don't understand. Elaine is nice to you, and you aren't even able to give her a simple answer? You said you understand English, right?"

"I no talk to women," the boy shot back.

Eric and Elaine looked at each other.

"Ah," said Eric, "it's probably a habit in your tribe. Kill them, yes, but talk to them, no."

"Yes," said the boy.

Elaine gave Eric a wide-eyed look.

"Okay, no problem," Eric said, "then I'll ask the questions and you answer straight to me. Is that clear? No games now. Let's get started. Your name?"

Silence.

Eric got up from the chair, and his body language told Elaine that the big guy was in no mood for playing nicely with the boy.

"Eric?" she said in a low tone. "Maybe if we take off his handcuffs, he'd agree to talk? Make a deal with him."

"The only deal I'm ready to make here..." Eric muttered.

For the first time, the boy looked at each of the officers in turn. Yet his face was still indifferent.

"Is that what you want?" Eric approached him. "If I release you from the handcuffs will you answer my questions?"

"Yes," he said simply, "but I speak only to you."

"It's okay, Eric," Elaine said, and before anyone could object, she had pulled a key from her belt and started to release the boy from the cuffs.

"Better?" she asked.

The boy released his hands. He looked at her and said nothing.

"What's your full name?" Eric asked again, "and no games now."

"Ahmed, but everyone calls me Hamdi."

"What's your last name?"

"We have no last names. It's our tribal name. We all belong to the same tribe," he said.

"Tribe Al-Miiarkh?" Eric asked.

"Yes," Hamdi answered.

"And where is this tribe located?"

"In Kalahari Desert, 1200 km from the Kilometer Zero stone."

Elaine's look at Eric told him she needed an explanation.

"We know it as the Zero Milestone but before there were precise maps and instruments to measure distance, they'd establish one main stone in the middle of the city and then measure the distance to where you live."

"Got it," she replied.

Eric turned back to Hamdi. "How old are you?"

"We don't have dates, but my mother says it's been 17 sun years since I was born."

"And who are the people in your immediate family?"

"Only my father, brother Jamal, and me."

"Do you have any sisters?"

"Yes, there are some, but we don't count them."

Elaine blushed with anger and sent Eric a withering glance.

"Very well, Hamdi. You see, so far everything is going fine. Now, just a few more questions and we're done for the night. Okay?"

Hamdi didn't respond.

"By the way," Eric asked, "out of curiosity, how did you learn English?

"You think because we don't live here we can't learn?" Hamdi replied and held Eric's stare. Hamdi continued, for once apparently happy to answer a question, "A few people of our tribe went to other places like England. When they come back, they teach us what they know and bring some books."

And there's the connection to the forged British passport, Eric thought, but said nothing. "Okay, never mind, we'll get back to that later."

He took a deep breath before continuing, "Let me ask you another question, are you married, Hamdi?"

Hamdi looked at Eric with a pain in his eyes. He lowered them to the table and said, "No."

Eric hesitated for a moment. Was he wrong? Wasn't Hamdi Leila's husband?

"Okay, Hamdi," said Eric. "We have a victim, a dead young woman, and we don't know why you killed her. Just tell us why you did it."

Hamdi was quiet and gazed at the table.

"Okay Hamdi, Just tell me what your motive was and we'll call it off for tonight and let you go back to your cell."

Although his line of questioning might seem basic, Eric knew he had to find out one thing, what Hamdi's motive was. Once he knew that, then it would be easy to establish if the child was still a potential target.

Still the boy said nothing.

"Hamdi, do you want us to call someone? Maybe a friend or a relative to come in? Maybe an attorney?" said Elaine

"NO! No one. No attorney!" The boy shouted back.

"Okay then, Hamdi. So just answer this one question for me. Why did you kill Leila?" said Eric.

Silence.

"Okay, Hamdi. What's it going to be? I don't have the whole night to waste on you. Just answer this one question and then you can get some sleep, and I," he added, "can go home and see my baby girls."

The boy's silence continued, but when Eric said the word 'girls,' he could have sworn he saw Hamdi flinch slightly.

"What happened, Hamdi? Does it bother you that I have two daughters that I'm crazy about, and to you they are worth nothing because they are girls? You don't count them as part of the family, right?"

Hamdi didn't respond, but simply closed his eyes.

Eric could sense that they were making some progress.

"You tired, boy? Had enough? Want to roll over and go to sleep?" Eric leaned menacingly forward before continuing. "What was the problem, Hamdi, wasn't Leila good enough for you? She didn't honor you? Is that why you cut her throat?"

Hamdi was quiet but it seemed that mentioning Leila had struck a nerve and, although he tried, he couldn't hold Eric's gaze.

Eric took a step back and heard Elaine let out a sigh of relief.

"Let's try again, shall we? I'll show you some photos and you can tell me what you see. All right?"

Eric pulled out a few of the photographs taken at the crime scene and a couple more from the morgue. In some of the images Leila's eyes were hollow, and in some they were closed. Her lips were pale, her skin looked bright and pure. It seemed like she was sleeping peacefully. Only in one picture though could you see her slashed throat.

Silence.

"Well? Not got anything to say?" Eric queried, peering into the young man's eyes.

Hamdi looked carefully at the pictures in front of him as if it was the first time he had ever seen Leila. He scanned the images, curiously looking over each one as if searching for something in particular. Then, using his finger, he traced over each image carefully.

"Well?" Eric asked again.

"Give him a minute," Elaine suggested.

Silence.

"Well?" Eric was impatient, and the tension was beginning to cut through him.

Hamdi picked up one photo. The one which clearly showed

the grotesque injury. Slowly he brought it forward before holding it tightly to to his face.

"Well, what do you know?" Eric said in a mocking tone. "Just that one picture out of all of them? What happened? You didn't like the rest of them? What do you think, Hamdi, that the color red suits her?"

Elaine could feel the tension in the room rising yet again. She wished that Hamdi would say something because Eric was far too close to this case.

Yet Hamdi still gazed in silence at the photo, seemingly unable to take his eyes off the deadly injury.

"Sssssss..." he said finally. "Very good, very good, Leila." Then he started to laugh. The sound resonated around the room, stunning even Eric into silence.

The laughter continued for at least a long minute until Eric finally cracked.

"Get him out of here!" Eric screamed furiously at the guard. "Throw this bastard into a cell and let him rot forever. I'll make sure you never see the light of day again!" he yelled at Hamdi as the guard cuffed him once again and led him, still laughing, out of the room.

"You will end up spending your life in jail!" Eric continued to shout into the corridor. "Do you hear me?! You're a son of a bitch! A baby killer!"

CHAPTER 28

From the darkest mind of a potential killer:

Two days after the wedding, Hamdi's body's temperature was very high.

He was placed in the women's tent. He was lying on the rug and hallucinating into the twilight. His mother and sisters worked hard to make him feel comfortable. They wiped his whole body with cold cloths and absorbed his sweat into a large ceramic vase. Time after time they replaced the wet cloth and poured ointment all over his body that stung the skin.

The tribe's elder spiritual whisperer, Miindilh, whispered a magic incantation and tried the best spells to remove the curse imposed by the gods.

"Liahiahiaiiii!" the voice rose in cry. "Holy and gracious gods. Please have mercy on this servant of yours, forgive for all his sins. Forgive for the ravages of evil and darkness. Raise this spirit and heed these wishes. Have pity and give it back its soul," she chanted.

Hamdi heard the chants of those who took the trouble to save him, but he couldn't move. Even to thank his sisters and mother was above his strength. His tongue was stuck, numb, and his throat made some gurgling noise and nothing else. He closed his eyes tightly. White light enveloped through the dark clouds. Led him to the gates of the underworld. Teetering between life and death. Between reality and illusion.

He let his thoughts disappear into the void. Darkness. The silence of death. Only a pair of lovely eyes peered at him. Enticing him to follow it. He heard giggles. He could see a gentle hand covering the mouth. He chuckled. Entranced by the sensuous lips. His body tensed. Eager for a touch. This passion filled his body.

Silence. He sank into the darkness. Something was shimmering in front of him. He got closer. Cautiously. It beckoned him to follow. He was curious. Following quietly. It led him into a cave. He had to bend down to cross the threshold. He heard a growl. He smelled danger. It sharpened his mind. Warned him, commanded him to escape. Too late. The Sa'eif was pulled against him. He stepped back but fell into the dark. He was blinded. Felt small stones rubbing his skin. He could taste the sand. He wanted to run away, but couldn't. Wanted to cry, but no sound came out. He whined. The monster snarled at him. It surrounded him in a circle. Smelled the fresh meat. The smell of his corpse. Its eyes were shining.

"Freeze!" He could hear his father's voice.

"Back away!"

"Do it like I taught you. Do it NOW!"

He wanted to. He wanted to live. His voice failed, and his hands were paralyzed.

Golden light surrounded him. Carrying him through the air. He was drifting outside the cave, out of danger.

He was burning up. He was rolling in sweat. Shivering from cold and fever. Chills twisted his body. He fainted and woke up several times.

The tribal messenger wanted to see Hamdi. His

voice was whispering, "Go toward the light, my child. Do not fight the mighty forces. They will guard you on this journey. Pray for your soul. Ask for forgiveness. Do it now!" He whimpered in the melody of lament and mourning. He heard his sisters joining in the lament. He knew that his time in this world was about to end.

"Liahiahiaiiiii!" the tribe's elder spiritual whisperer raised her voice and cried out to the spirits. "Mercy," her voice carried up to heaven. She raised her head and put smelling salts next to his nose. Terrible odor filled his lungs and choked him, causing him to gasp for air. He woke up. Opened his eyes. He could hear a voice filling the air. "Come to me my love, come..." blood red lips whispered.

He begged. One more time. Please. Before his soul returned to the sky.

He shivered. Turned over. He had to get up. He was so weak. The tent pole helped him pull his weight up. ...Must comply.

"No, don't go," his mother cried.

"I must ..." he whispered, "see her face ... touch it ... stroke her hair." He barely rose. Falling back on his knees. Lips whispered in his ears, "Come to me, my love." It was tempting. He felt his

body stiffen. His passion for the desired one.
The sand scorched his flesh. He crawled on his
stomach. He did not give up. Slithering like a
snake. He felt the sun hitting him and pulling
him to go outside. It stung his eyes. The distance
between the women's tent and the new couple's
tent seemed endless. He was sipping his own
saliva. Past and present intertwine. His mouth
felt dry as if he has walked in the desert for 40
years.

Never give up. He was so close. So drenched in
sweat.

Keep going.

Keep coming.

"Water," he begged, "I need water to quench my
thirst."

He collapsed. Hallucinating into the darkness.

He was calm. No longer thirsty nor hungry. He
was with the gods. He smiled from his death.
Leila was there with him. They were together at
last. He felt her warm touch on his body. The
heat of the bodies. So soft.

My Leila, my desired one, my love. "I traveled
and came to you," he whispered. "Hold me, my
love. Give me time to lie down on your lap. I

would rather die a thousand times over next to you than be alive without you. Now we are united."

Eyes were smiling. The hands were taking off the garment rags that covered his body. Veils and Jellabiya were slipping off.

Black hair blew in the desert wind. Fingers were kissed, one finger at a time.

Soft and red lips. Drown in the gaze.

Hamdi shuddered.

The light covered him, and the breeze carried him up to a golden sky at dusk. It felt like floating. Like oobserving the desert from a distance. The women's lamenting voices approached him, tried to get him back, to disconnect him from his love.

He refused. Struggled. Insisted. He begged. Please, leave us. Let us stay together. We belong here.

He gave up.

The noises surrounded him. Screamed in his ears.

Eyes opened in alarm.

Meet other scared eyes.

Nine months later Leila gave birth to a baby girl.

CHAPTER 29

I looked at my friends and kept quiet. I hesitated.

"I had a dream," I confessed finally.

"Sounds interesting. Somewhat familiar." A mocking smile draped over Rob's lips.

"What was your dream?" Miriam asked.

"If I tell you, you'll think I'm crazy."

"We already think you're crazy," Rob said chuckling, "and you won't be able to surprise us no matter how many exercises you'll come up with."

We all laughed.

"I dreamt that I was in a huge conference hall. The floor was covered with a red carpet and with ornate chandeliers hanging from the ceiling. The room was full of people in business attire. There were reporters and photographers walking with their equipment everywhere. Everybody rushed to get closer to the stage. On the stage were three tables. Next to each table were some people. I couldn't see their faces.

I pushed my way through the crowd to get closer to the stage. I tried to peek between reporter's shoulders and their giant microphones that blocked access. Suddenly, next to the main table, I saw a strange man. I had a hunch that I knew him, but had no idea from where. He was wearing a gray suit and a red bow tie. He looked embarrassed, like he didn't belong there.

Then suddenly the man in the gray suit timidly approached the microphone. He cleared his throat. Nobody noticed. He was extremely shy. Then he pulled a comb out of his pocket and started combing his shaggy gray hair.

"Excuse me," he whispered into the microphone and coughed.

People kept talking.

"Hello, may I please..." he tried again.

Suddenly, my boss Meredith appeared in front of the mic. She placed her hand on his shoulder to encourage him. She grabbed the microphone and said, "I'm going to count to three. When I get to number three, I expect silence!"

At once it was quiet. No one moved.

Then it hit me. I remembered. This is Zachariah, our maintenance worker in school. Wasn't he supposed to retire by now?"

Everyone laughed. "A strange dream," Drew commented. "Luckily I'm not Dr. Freud and don't need to decode your dream." We laughed again.

"I have a feeling that this is not the end of the dream," said

Rob as a grin returned to his lips.

"Yes. There's more," I said. Everyone looked at me again.

"So then, reporters approached him, Zachariah, and pushed their microphones under his nose. One reporter asked him, 'How exactly did you, out of everyone, do it? Are you some kind of a genius?'

"Zachariah said nothing. He just looked at me. He looked at me straight into the eyes. Not a word came out of his mouth. Then it hit me.

"Zachariah slowly raised his hand and without avoiding my gaze pointed at me. Then he whispered, "'It's all because of your drowning tree in the mud.'" Then, I woke up."

"Wow, that's weird," said Kenny. "Basically, what you're saying, if I understand it correctly, is that *The Pencil Pro* causes people to be geniuses, but also become somewhat crazy."

"Interesting," said Drew. "Actually I see something else here. I interpret his dream as our mission to give equal opportunity to ordinary people to think like leaders, so that ideas can come from anyone."

"The main question here," said Miriam, "at least the way I see it, is whether you, with your exercises, can create the reality or just change the way we perceive reality as it is."

"Great question," Cheryl noted.

"There is a very well-known approach in the education field called self-fulfilling prophecy," I said. "Actually, it's not just related to education. It's in every aspect of life, but I first heard about it in an education intro course as a freshman in college.

"The idea refers to the process by which I have expectations from another person or from myself, which makes me unconsciously behave in accordance with those expectations.

"Let's say there's a teacher who taught your class last year. He wants to give you some guidelines about the students who will attend your class this year. He mentions who the weak students are and who the stronger ones are. If you follow his recommendation, and you treat students the 'expected' way, you actually prevent them the opportunity to make any change. They simply will adapt to your expectations. Studies have shown that if you refer to the weak students as weak, they will fulfill what is predicted, while the stronger students, from whom you expect to continue to excel, and thus challenge them more than the others, would probably succeed as expected. You actually 'fixed' the situation and did not give everyone an equal opportunity."

"So, what you are saying," Cheryl queried, "is that you could create reality? If I'm looking for a parking space in a crowded garage, it may suddenly become vacant? And if I'm dreaming of a beautiful garden full of flowers in the middle of winter it could happen?"

"Not exactly," I replied. "But if you think of a long-term goal and take small steps toward your target, you will be able to make your dream come true. If you want beautiful flowers in the winter you should build a greenhouse. Begin with a small warm tent, then add the right equipment that is suitable for your needs, and one day you'll get to pick the flowers."

"Okay, so what other situations or real-life problems can you help me solve, based on your creative thinking?" Cheryl asked.

"Good question," I smiled. "Let's think about this, shall we?"

∞CR

"Good morning, students," I said as I walked into class the following Monday morning. "Today we're going to try something different."

"What do you mean something different?" they asked.

"I'll explain. You know that at least until now, the exercises that I brought into class were mostly theoretical or stories I made up myself, in order to help us practice and sharpen our minds."

"Okay," the students said, trying to guess my intentions. "And today?"

"So, this time, I did something a little bit different. I actually searched real-life problems that people posted on this 'ask the experts' website. I copied it and brought them in as they were originally written by real people. Today we are going to pretend we're the experts and suggest real-life solutions using nothing but our creative thinking power. Are you ready? Let's try **Exercise No. 10.**"

EXERCISE NO. 10

Read the following instructions:

The next exercise will focus on solving real-life situations with the power of our creative thinking. Not every problem can be solved immediately or brought to a complete solution, but we can find ways to deal with the problems and move toward solving them. For example, a homeless person will not become rich in one day (no, it's not about winning the lottery), but if he attends free evening courses or does good deeds to improve the environment, he may have a chance to change his situation.

In this exercise, we'll present a basic situation. You serve as the advisor.

How can you help these people determine their destination? What steps do they need to take in order to reach the desired goal? Remember, money does not grow on trees. None of our people are about to win the lottery. Try to help them find realistic alternatives.

Turn on your thinking cap and think outside the box. Good luck!

Scene No. 1

Jacob loves his job. He worked at the same hi-tech company for the past 12 years. He could never trade this job for any other one in the area. His CEO appreciates him and his knowledge.

The other employees are great too. Jacob is happy. What more can he ask for? He receives generous bonuses on projects that he manages successfully and days off for personal reasons when he needs them.

There is only one problem, a huge problem that causes Jacob to be frustrated. Traffic.

Jacob's house is located not more than 17 miles from the company's offices. Seemingly, a reasonable driving distance.

If Jacob were driving to work on Sundays, for example, when the roads are empty, it wouldn't probably take him more than 25 minutes.

However, due to traffic congestion and traffic jams, the average travel time each day is an hour to cross the bridge to his workplace.

Jacob is frustrated. He tried everything, leave an hour earlier, leave an hour later. Nothing worked. There's only one bridge that crosses that road.

He cannot move out from the house, in which he, Tracey, and their four children live. They invested so much time and money to make this place homey.

And he cannot he even think about leaving his workplace.

Please help Jacob. What can Jacob do in order to solve this problem?

CHAPTER 30

From the darkest mind of a potential killer:

Hamdi was the first one to figure it out.

It was enough for him to look into her eyes and see.

He didn't say anything. He's not stupid. He can keep secrets. Even if they beat him with a whip.

They only beat up women in our tribe. Women and children. Never men.

No way!

The girl grew up before our eyes.

He was angry. He was furious. How did we get in that problem? Who seduced who? We remembered the charmed looks. We remembered the soft skin and the red lips. But now? Every time he passes by, in front of the newlyweds' tent, he lowers his eyes. Buries his look into the sand dunes.

It's no longer pretty. Only black veil that covers everything but the dark eyes. Long black dresses that drape the body down to the feet. Even the feet that peek through the dress don't lure him any longer.

Jamal was not happy with his new baby girl. Never mind, we assured him, next time it will be a boy. We promised.

Then, one day Jamal just realized.

Jamal just came to the tent and went berserk.

At first we didn't understand what took over him. Where did this evil spirit come from?

Jamal screamed. His eyes rolled. We were afraid. Something must have happened to him. The other men ran away, leaving just the two brothers. Jamal pulled his hair and called the gods out of anger, out of despair. Finally, he laid down on his face and wept. They both cried, pleaded, and denied everything.

"Jamal, you are my life. I love you more than my own life. You are my brother. What can I do?" said Hamdi.

Jamal calmed down. It seems as if the evil power had left him. He looked tired. Exhausted.

"I am the firstborn in this family," Jamal hissed between his lips. "I bring only boys. But only the second son, only the second can make girls!"

Hamdi cried again. He got down on his knees in front

of Jamal. "It wasn't me," he whispered.

Jamal was lost. He wiped his tears with the back of his hand and then slowly stood up.

What would he do now?

Jamal approached Hamdi slowly, but determined. Boldly, without shaking, Jamal pulled the Sa'eif and held it to Hamdi's neck.

He cursed him. Wished for his brother's death.

Hamdi closed his eyes. He was Jamal's prisoner.

"Do with me what you wish," he whispered.

The sword was in his hand. It burned Hamdi's neck. Another prayer to the gods.

Slowly Jamal returned the Sa'eif back to its place. He changed his mind.

"I want to take another wife. A lot of women...they will give me boys."

Jamal relaxed.

Silence. There were no more words to be said. The brothers wiped their tears while their faces filled with grains of golden sand.

Just before Jamal left the tent he looked back and said, "You, make sure to disappear. And take this girl of yours, too. After all, I'm the older son. The rights were given to me. I am the sovereign. Do you understand?"

CHAPTER 31

"I brought you some coffee," Elaine said handing him a cup.

Eric raised a quizzical look, "Elaine?"

"Yes, Eric?"

"What if we're wrong, what if Hamdi isn't really a killer?"

"What do you mean?" Elaine pulled out a chair and sat down.

"Let's assume for a moment that Hamdi is a good man," he said.

"What?"

"Let's just assume it for a moment. Can a good man kill his woman and threaten her daughter?

"Let's assume that he planted those clues of a blonde wig at the murder scene. Maybe his whole story is a lie. Why would someone do that?"

"Maybe someone wants us to know that the victim has a false identity. Someone wanted us to reveal the secret?"

"Okay." The wheels were turning in his head. "But what if someone planted hidden clues so we can figure them out and discover where they came from. And do you remember the note with the address that the Chinese women handed me when she and Louisa came for the first time to the police station? I'm not really sure now if it was her handwriting or someone else's. Someone who wanted me to know about the girl."

"Okay," said Elaine. "So let's move on with this same line of thinking and say that Hamdi is a good person and he is the one who planted the clues that would lead us to look for him, and he certainly knew the police were tracking down Louisa's home so if he comes over he will be sure to get caught."

"True," said Eric. "I'm trying to get into the mind of the killer for 24 hours. Let's say I knew what my mission would be and I knew my victim. That I knew I had to commit the crime not on the land of my tribe. Me or someone else was planning this move for me. I was following my victim without her knowing it. Maybe I was forced to do that. Maybe someone challenged me or put a lot of pressure on me to kill her. I am familiar with the murder weapon and know how to use it. I know her routines. Now, everything is ready. All that was missing was my courage."

"Fine, Eric. Let's say that someone else encouraged you to do this, forget about encouraging, pushing you to do it, forcing you to. Threatens that if you don't do it something bad would happen to you. What's next?"

"Okay." Eric took back the reins. "So I have a goal and let's say I got my courage and I did it. I cut her, beheaded her. What next? I have a girl to kill. I've already started the killing journey, why should I stop now? Why wait? Why should I lose my chance? What changed all of a sudden?"

"That's interesting, Eric. "So let's start for a second from the end. We have a victim with a false identity, a little girl who is alive, and someone named Hamdi behind bars. What are we looking for right now? Motive?"

"Yes, I'm looking for an answer to the question, why. Why murder Leila in the first place? Why did he come to us so we can get him behind bars? Why did he plant clues at the scene so we can trace her false identity and the secret that Leila is hiding?"

"Okay, if I take it from there, Eric, I would ask what was the hidden message. I assume the obvious message is that he wanted to kill Leila by beheading her. What's the underlying message here? What secret is he hiding from us?"

Eric sighed. "Elaine, I have to admit that I have no answers, but I like the direction this is heading...and I think I have an idea."

An hour later Eric and Elaine went to the detention cell with the release papers in his hands.

The guard hurried to open the gate.

"Come with me," Eric said to Hamdi. "You're released."

"What?" asked Hamdi, his eyes widening in surprise.

"Get out," Eric said. "Get out of here."

Hamdi scrambled to his feet but didn't move.

"Well? Come on, get out of here," Eric repeated, "before I change my mind."

Hamdi looked around. It seemed as if he could not believe it. He was afraid to make a sound.

Eric began to feel the anger surge within him. "What the hell is wrong with you? Can't you hear me? What's your problem? Do I need to call the interpreter?"

"No," Hamdi whispered.

"What?" Eric yelled furiously. "Are you crazy? I'm running around for hours to get you the release papers and that's how you thank me? You ungrateful son of a bitch. In two seconds I'm going to leave you here and lock the door for good. Do you hear me? You'll never get out of here. Do you understand?"

"Yes, I understand," Hamdi whispered. "And I don't care. I'm not going out. I stay here." He sat down again and covered his face with his hands.

Eric looked as if he was about to explode.

"Eric, give me a minute," Elaine said, and sat on the bench next to Hamdi. She was careful not to lay a hand on his shoulder.

"Hamdi, what's going on? Tell me," she asked softly.

Hamdi lifted his eyes and looked at her with true desperation.

"I can't." He covered his face with his hands.

"Why not?"

"I promised her," he whispered. "I promised Leila. We...we had...honor agreement."

Eric and Elaine looked at each other, confused.

"Promised her what?" Eric asked gently.

"I loved Leila, I really did," his voice cracked. "We pretended that we hate each other...but it was no true. My brother, Jamal, he told me to kill her. You'll never understand."

"What will we never understand?" asked Eric.

"There's nothing in your world like this. No honor to your tribe here. It is something strong. More than life. If your brother say kill, you kill," his voice sounded lost.

"So did you really kill Leila?" Elaine asked.

Hamdi burst into tears. "I loved Leila so much. I was 13 years and she was 12 when we met. Just kids. She understood everything. She loved me too, but the families...they'd never say yes...we wanted to get married. She was given to my brother. Jamal married her. He is older, so he has the rights. You understand? And she...she was just a girl, a property, she can't say no... the family decides for her."

"So what did you do, Hamdi?" asked Elaine.

"We made a deal, Leila and me. She understood. I had to prove that I'm loyal to my family. Leila knew she had to die. We made a cut in our fingers and put our blood together. It was her idea. She said that first I kill her, then my family would be happy, and if they take me to jail then..."

"You'll be able to save the girl? That Louisa will be alive?" Eric closed his eyes and leaned his head against the wall.

"Yes. Because if I'm in jail, my family knows that I kept my promise and I honor the tribe. That I did the right thing. That I did what they said."

"What about Louisa? What about the men who came here to check that you did it? Wouldn't they look for her?" Eric asked.

"No! No one knows. They think she died with her mother, that I threw her body to the river. I swore to them. I gave them my word of honor!"

Elaine and Eric exchanged a glance.

"Please," Hamdi pleaded. "Louisa has a fake name. Her real name is Mawiyah, which means 'the nature of life.' No one in my family knows that her name is Louisa now."

"Certainly," said Eric. "No one will ever know."

"What about you?" asked Elaine.

"I must stay in jail," Hamdi insisted. "If you take me out of here, my family will look for me. The gods will punish me. I have to stay in jail, you understand? I promised Leila to save our little girl. I can't go back home."

Eric and Elaine exchanged glances again. "Well," Eric finally said. "I'll see what I can do."

"Hamdi, one last question," asked Elaine as she and Eric stood up, "Who really killed Leila?"

Hamdi chuckled, "Leila did it. She always had more power than me. Not as strong as a man, but emotionally she was so strong like she could fly to the sky. She was like a beast protecting her child. To give up her life meant nothing...it was Leila's plan."

CHAPTER 32

From the darkest mind of an innocent killer

A precise cut. Slaughter of the neck.
Like an animal that doesn't resist its end. Aware
of its fate. Just like cutting a paper with scissors.
The knife in the hands of an artist. Leather trim,
cut throat, and a slashed neck.
It is not me. I am innocent.
I slaughter animals. I slash wild beasts, cut off
their heads before I prepare them for dinner. I
do not look them in the eyes even though I feel
nothing. Soon there will be a pile of flesh and
bones, nothing else.
They sent him to kill. What could I say? They are
his family.

My husband Jamal and his brother Hamdi.

They gave him a Sa'eif and said: Go! Kill! It is no more than killing a beast. No more.

What could I do?

I am better with a sword.

The loyalty to your family stands above all. That's how they taught us. Respect your family, honor your tribal name.

Without our tribe's name that was given to us by the previous generations, there's no reason for life. The gods see it all and take revenge on those who do not stand by their families. You can smell their incense everywhere. They know. They see. They are watching from above.

His family arranged everything. Jamal woke him up one night. He came to Hamdi's tent and called him to follow. It was dark and cold in the desert. Just us and the shirt on our skin. They put us on a horse and gave Hamdi the rope of the animal on which we rode. All of us.

We went quietly. Two older men joined us. I didn't know them. They didn't talk to me, not even once. I heard that they speak English very well. They took care of all the papers and the money. They gave us food and water and told us where to sleep. That's all.

We were silent. We knew what was waiting ahead and did not resist. Like animals we accepted our fate. They knew we could not be sacrificed within the tribe. That the secret had to be kept. And though there were words between us, they were not spoken. We walked in silence for hours, we could hear the sound of horses' hooves. Then the two men took us to an airplane. The transport of the so-called civilized world. They gave us papers to give to the officials. Everything seemed to move so fast and yet so slow. There was light, then dark. It was cold, then too hot. Shadows surrounded us. We slept most of the time. Before we left, Jamal gave him something to swallow. He said: "Take it. It gives you courage." He took it. We slept and slept. The whole time.

Screams woke me up suddenly. The two men took the girl away. Tore her from my arms. We'll return her later, they said. But we knew they would not. I screamed like a wild beast who protects her young cub. They gave me a strong slap. It took many more to make me silent.

And then we were here. America.

They put us in two separate closed apartments and sent me to work cleaning floors. They told the Asian landlord not to mention that he saw us, ever. They threatened that they will kill him if he would say a word.

They put him in another apartment and gave us mattresses. We were both there, in the building, the child was there too, but our eyes never met. I was still difficult, so to keep me quiet, they gave me the child back. I promised not to say a word. Not to talk to anybody. I promised to tell the child that her family was dead, that her father was dead, that Uncle Hamdi was dead. That everyone is ghost now. That the tribe no longer existed.

They gave us water, food, and pills to swallow every day. "It will make you stronger," they said. We swallowed and stayed in the dark. They gave me and my child clothes so we would not attract attention. There were blond wigs too. It didn't match the smooth darkness of our skin.

Then one morning it happened. They pushed Hamdi off the mattress.

"Now!" they screamed at him. "Do it now!"

They placed his sword in his hands, or maybe it was another steel blade knife? I don't remember. They told him to hide it under his shirt inside a special carrying bag so that no one can see. The same Sa'eif that he used to slaughter beasts. "Go!

NOW! Do it for the sake of your own dignity, your loyalty to your family. She's waiting for you, under the bridge."

He walked in the street. Blurred. He swallowed three pills together to give him courage like Jamal said.

I had more courage.

It was cold, but he was sweating and his shirt clung closely to him. He walked, not certain of what he was doing or why he was doing it. The sword banged heavy against his chest.

He heard screaming in his head.

"Slaughter this slut," screamed his brother Jamal.

"Kill her like a beast," cried his father.

"Save us," begged his mother. "Save your family's honor and dignity. Save our tribal name!"

"Everything is up to you, my son," said his father, "prove to us your loyalty," he cried.

Cars whizzed by him. Brakes screeched and horns were blaring as he walked. He had no idea where he was.

The smell of frying oil filled his nostrils. That's all he remembered. The smell of oil. Letters danced before his eyes. Yellow neon signs, or maybe it was green? Lights going on and off.

The myriad symbols scribbled on the paper in my hand. The plan was laid out.

Many people walked toward him. Everything was spinning. They pushed him to the side. He felt like a pendulum. Pushing, falling, and standing up again. Searching his way in the dark.

Then he saw me. He knocked into me before keeping on walking. Our eyes met. He saw my veil falling from my head, hovering for a moment in the air and then falling on the ground. It was heavy, almost as a concrete stone. It crushed him. We were back in the desert.

He could barely get out of there. He got up and started running. The Sa'eif was under his shirt. I think. I don't remember. Maybe it was another kind of knife? "STOP. You can't run away from me!" I thought I screamed.

I yelled. I think I did. Was it real? Was I dreaming? I can't tell. His eyes were frightened. He ran away. My pulse quickened. I chased him and then reached out my hand and grabbed him. He stopped under the bridge. He looked around. He had nowhere to escape. Like a deer in the network of tigers. He trembled. So beautiful. So pure and innocent.

I grabbed my throat. He closed his eyes. Accepting the fate.

"Remember," I whispered, "save our child, the fruit of our love."

Just for a split second I hesitated. Should I go for the cut or stab?

I said nothing. I couldn't move. The street was spinning very fast. I closed my eyes. What am I doing? Killing a human being? Me?!

"This is just a beast," Jamal was whispering in his ear. His voice was full of hatred. "Go for the throat. Cut it."

"Prepare her for dinner," his father cried.

"Our honor!" cried his mother.

I closed my eyes as tight as I could. He didn't want to hear anything. Not to see anything. Not to think. Clean the poison away from him.

He lost the feeling in his hands.

But I was strong enough to grab the knife from his hand turn my back to him and revel in the release of my sins as I put the knife to my own throat.

Hamdi woke up.

I was lying on the ground next to him.

I am Leila, and that was my story .

CHAPTER 33

Cheryl's and Drew's wedding was held on Sunday morning. Cheryl dreamed of a big wedding, and Drew wanted something modest. They settled somewhere in the middle. Drew claimed that weddings inside an air-conditioned hall will be preferable; Cheryl wanted a blooming garden wedding among beautiful flowers.

A compromise was offered. The wedding ceremony would be held in the garden and immediately after the ceremony, the guests would be invited into the air-conditioned hall.

Cheryl wore a white dress with long sleeves. Drew was wearing a white suit. After the ceremony he removed his tie.

A modest crowd of about 80 people came to congratulate and celebrate with the couple. A band called "Skulls in Paradise" was on stage and played their greatest hits. An hour later there were toasts and speeches in honor of the couple.

The bride's father gave a moving speech and wished his daughter to fulfill her dream to reach the top of Kilimanjaro with her partner. Drew's parents said that "a third marriage is a charm." Then it was my turn to speak.

I went up to the stage and took the microphone from Drew's father's hands.

"Cheryl and Drew, dear families and dear guests," I read from the page. "I remember the day that Drew and I met for the very first time. I was in second grade, a cute and shy boy. The teacher placed my seat next to Drew's, and my life was changed...but not for the best..." I paused and heard laughter.

"Drew is not just a childhood friend, he's more like my second brother. Maybe a third brother after Kenny, whom I met in first grade, or fourth brother, after my sister married Rob, who became my brother-in-law. In fact, from a single boy with one sister, suddenly I had an extended family.

"As a family member, I can tell those who are not familiar with Drew as much as I am, that Drew has many positive qualities; let's count a few of them...ummm, on second thought...let's move on to Cheryl." It was nice to hear people laugh. I knew that Drew appreciated the humor.

"Even before I met you, Cheryl, I was told by Drew what a lovely woman you are. He told me your favorite aroma is the smell of wet grass after a rainfall. That you know how to use Google to find how many Labrador dogs there are in Brazil, and between yoga lessons you have time to think of a bread-cutting machine."

We exchanged sweet smiling glances between Drew, Cheryl, Rob, Kenny, and me.

"In conclusion, I would like to offer some tips to our couple. First tip, if you walk down the street and see a drowning tree in mud, wait. Don't rush in to help it. Maybe the rain needs to reinforce its point of view.

Tip number two, do not judge a book by its cover. Remember that the book is more than just a story that begins at the end.

Tip number three, beware of old women. Perhaps they are hiding a secret code at the train station. Also, I recommend paying special attention to maintenance guys named Zachariah..."

I paused. People listened politely to me. It is doubtful whether anyone understood what I meant, except for those involved in our project.

"And now seriously," I continued. "This morning I read an article in the newspaper about a murder case that was solved recently in Rhode Island. It was only one detective's initiative to find the truth. I think his name was Eric Gutenheim or something like that. At the end of the interview he said something that I found to be very interesting. He said: 'Don't hit rock bottom, just go sideways'...which means that if you're stuck with no solution, just look for alternatives because you could miss the entire truth by not looking from every angle.

"If there's anything I can advise you and to all the people here today is to follow your dreams to be successful. Do not give up. Ask questions and don't take things for granted. Always think that there's a third option; that the world is not black and white, right-click or left click. Remember, we have the power to change reality, to change the way we see the world across the spectrum and discover new things. Let your mind run wild. Encourage and practice it to think and to generate "aha" moments. If you have something that you really want to achieve, go ahead and do it! Find the courage in you. Your dream can change many people's reality.

"The power to create your reality is in your hands. I wish the wonderful couple lots of success and happiness down the road. I love you both."

I folded the paper and tucked it into the pocket of my shirt. I rushed to kiss Cheryl on the cheeks and to hug Drew. "Thank you, my brother," Drew whispered.

"Congrats." I hugged Drew's and Cheryl's parents. Miriam hugged me back when I returned to my chair.

"Excellent speech, little brother," she whispered.

"Thank you, sis."

"I liked how you mentioned *The Pencil Pro*. Drew and Cheryl smiled all the time and others listened."

"There is something here, Miriam. I can't explain it, but I feel it. There's something stronger here, and I hate to leave it just between us."

"So don't do it, Adam. Don't keep it as a secret between you, your YouTube viewers, and your Facebook fans. Share it with everyone."

Miriam went back to sip from her glass of champagne, and I went back to my thoughts.

When I got back home that night, a little dizzy from the alcohol, I couldn't fall asleep. My thoughts gave me no rest.

I placed the laptop on my knees and I began to write. I wrote and wrote and wrote...

Acknowledgements

I would like to express my gratitude to a large number of people who saw me through this book; to all those who provided support, read, wrote, offered comments, allowed me to quote their remark, and shared their insight, wisdom and creativity with me.

I would like to thank my special friend and editor, Hal Gordon, for the ongoing support. Hal's dedication, as well as his wisdom, made this book a successful one. Hal, you are truly a good friend.

This book couldn't have been completed without the talent and the devotion of an incredible editor, Bobby Brower. Bobby contributed his mind and soul into shaping the parallel stories as well as the characters.

I'd like to extend my appreciation to many professionals who assisted in the editing, proofreading and designing. Special thanks to ARI, Judi Blitz, Karen Thompson and Jennifer Boyer.

Last and not least: I'm grateful for the support of my closest friends and family. My parents who taught me that it's okay to be different, to be curious, to voice my doubts, not to be afraid to ask and never accept things for granted.

To my sister, Miki, my nieces and nephews, Gal, Noy, Yam and Jen, thank you for always supporting me on my journey.

A special thanks to you, Shoko.

To my kids, whose ongoing love and support are more than I could ever have asked for. Shachar and Kiki - you are my inspiration, you are making my world complete.

Finally, to you Kobi, my life partner, who supported me through the process, tolerated my frustrations as well as celebrated my success. Thank you for being there for me.

I beg forgiveness of all those who have been with me over the course of the years and whose names I have failed to mention.

The Pencil Pro presents:

Open the box and let your ideas fly... A playful thought-provoking card game to stimulate your creative thinking

toolit – Be a Creative Thinker!

A new world of entertainment constructed from real-life situations and decisions you must make. No true or false answers, no limitations.

The only answer is your creative thinking.

Pull a card, think outside the box as you work to solve challenges and jump start your imagination.

Play the game by yourself, with your friends, or family.

toolit can be used to interview a potential candidate for a job or start a mind-provoking group conversation. The options are endless!

NOW AVAILABLE ON AMAZON.COM

www.ingramcontent.com/pod-product-compliance
Lightning Source LLC
Chambersburg PA
CBHW021511240626
47154CB00002B/589